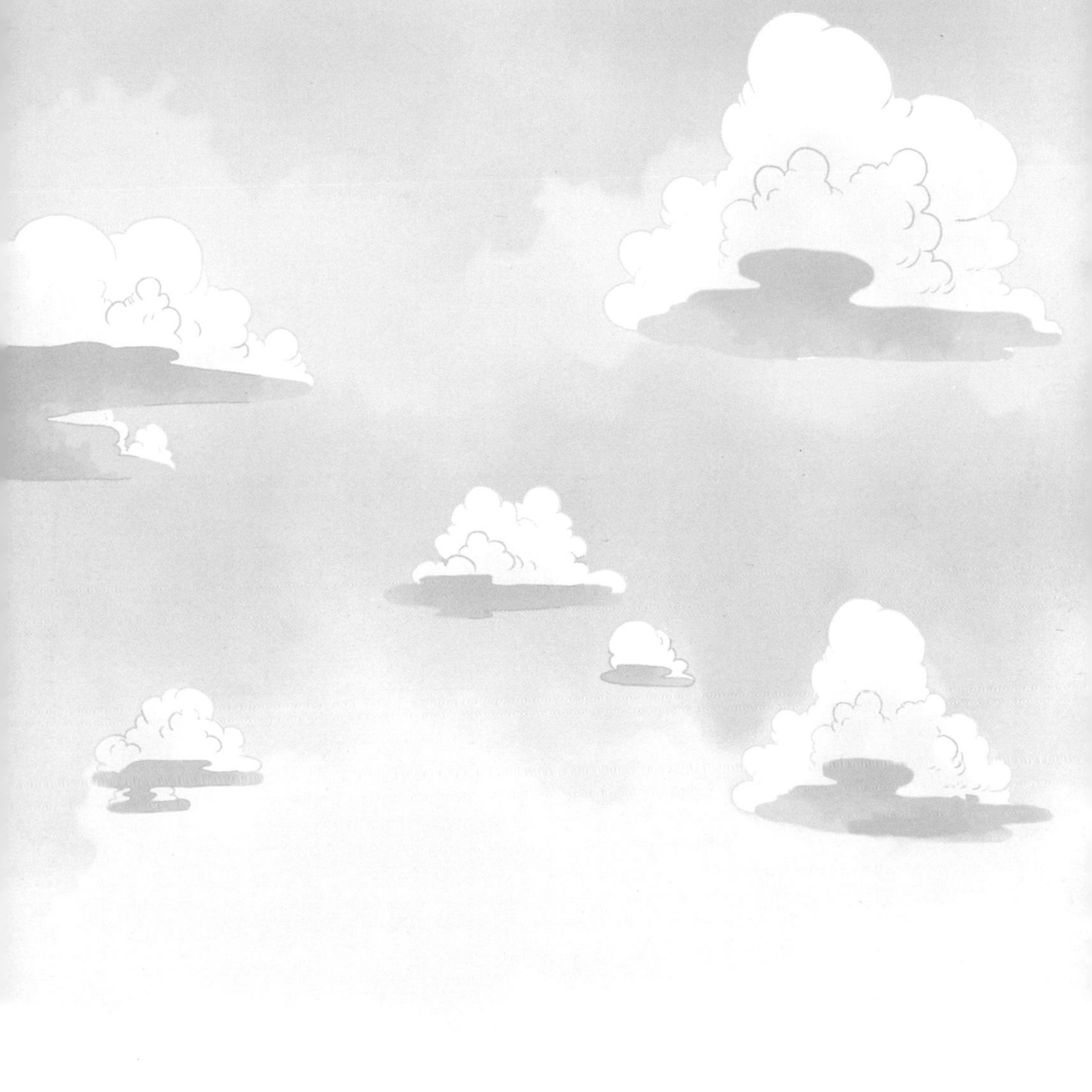

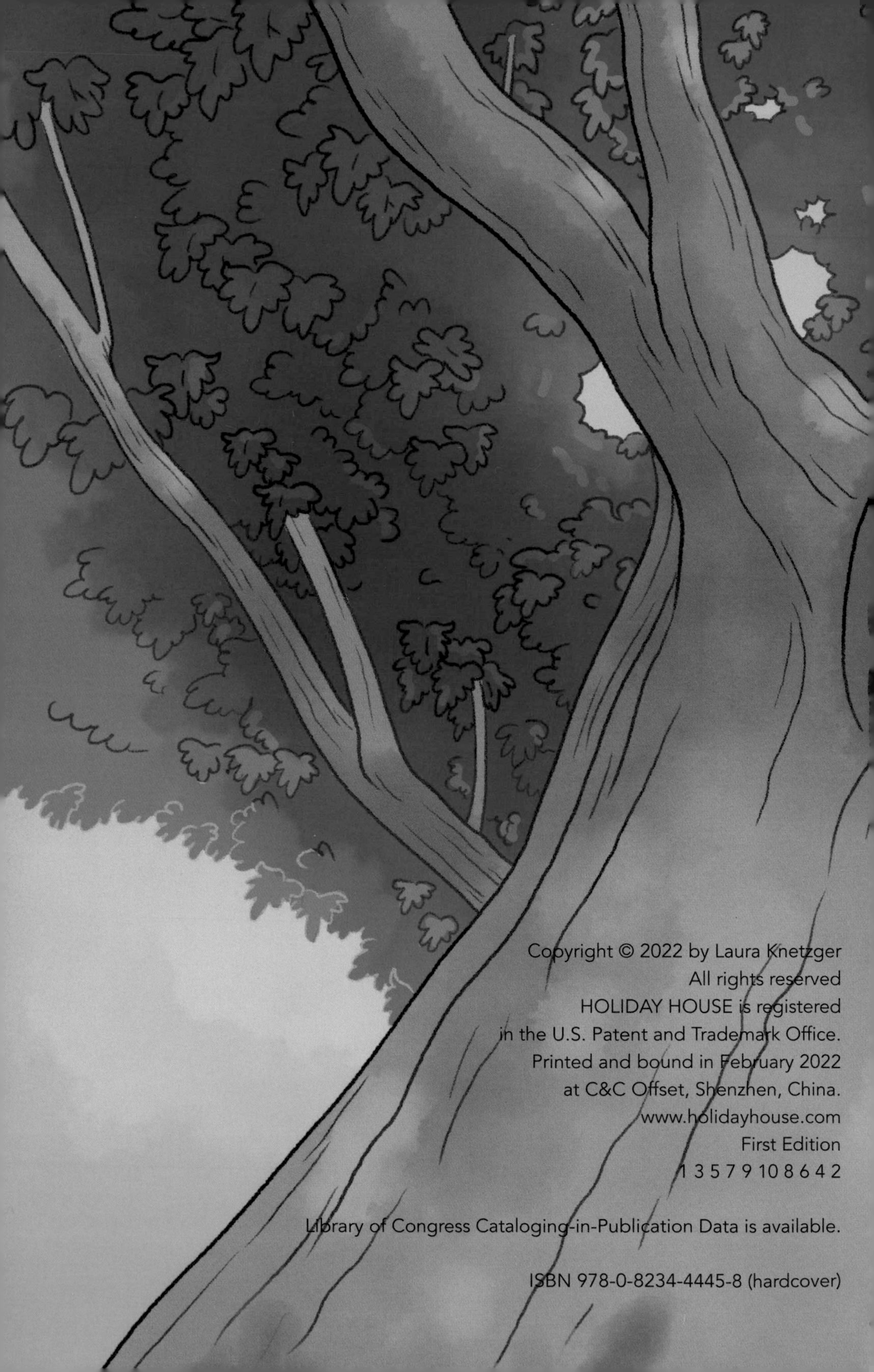


HOLIDAY HOUSE is registered
in the U.S. Patent and Trademark Office.
Printed and bound in February 2022
at C&C Offset, Shenzhen, China.
www.holidayhouse.com
First Edition
1 3 5 7 9 10 8 6 4 2

Library of Congress Cataloging-in-Publication Data is available.

ISBN 978-0-8234-4445-8 (hardcover)

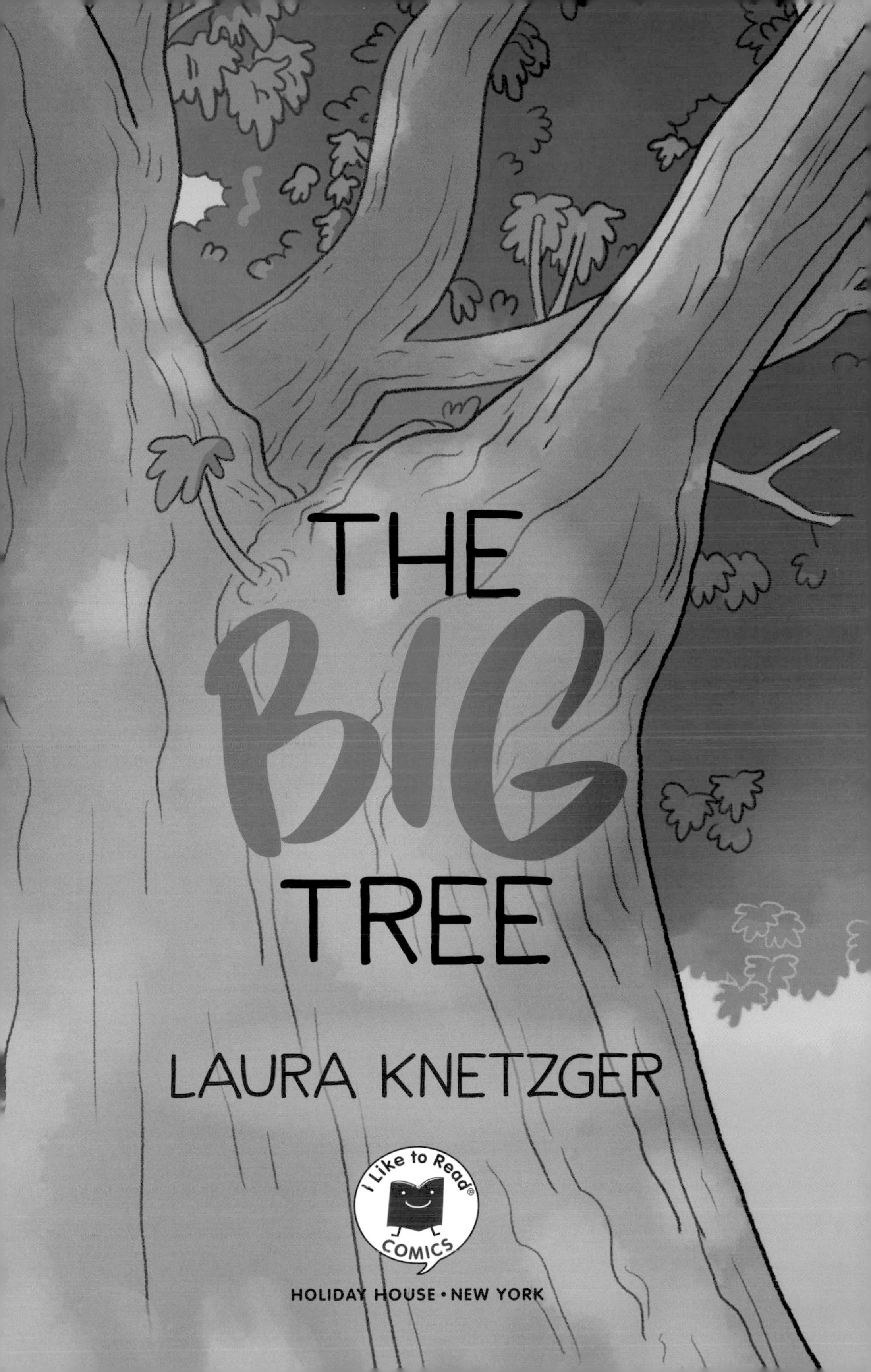

# THE BIG TREE

LAURA KNETZGER

I Like to Read® COMICS

HOLIDAY HOUSE • NEW YORK

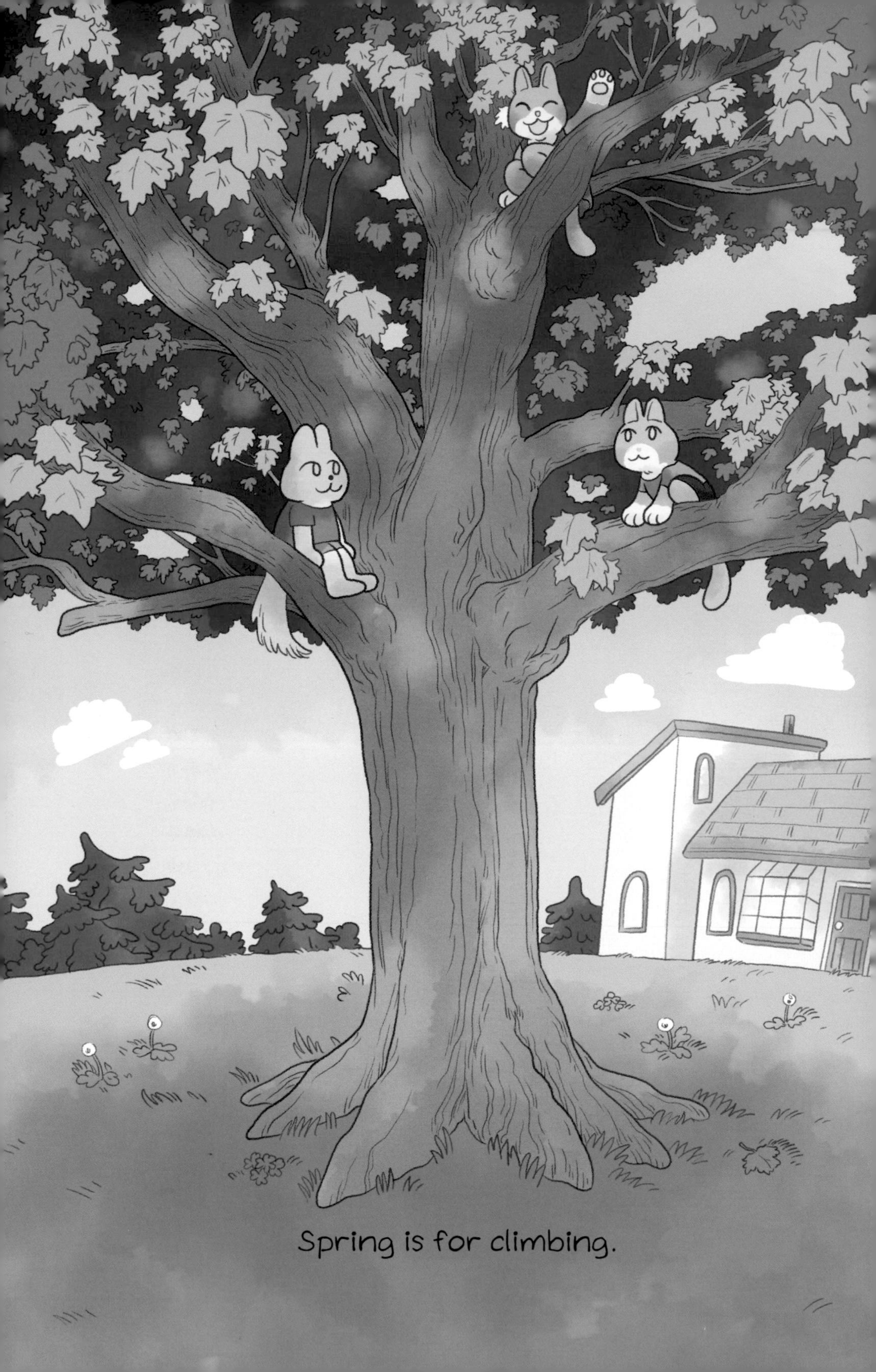

Spring is for climbing.

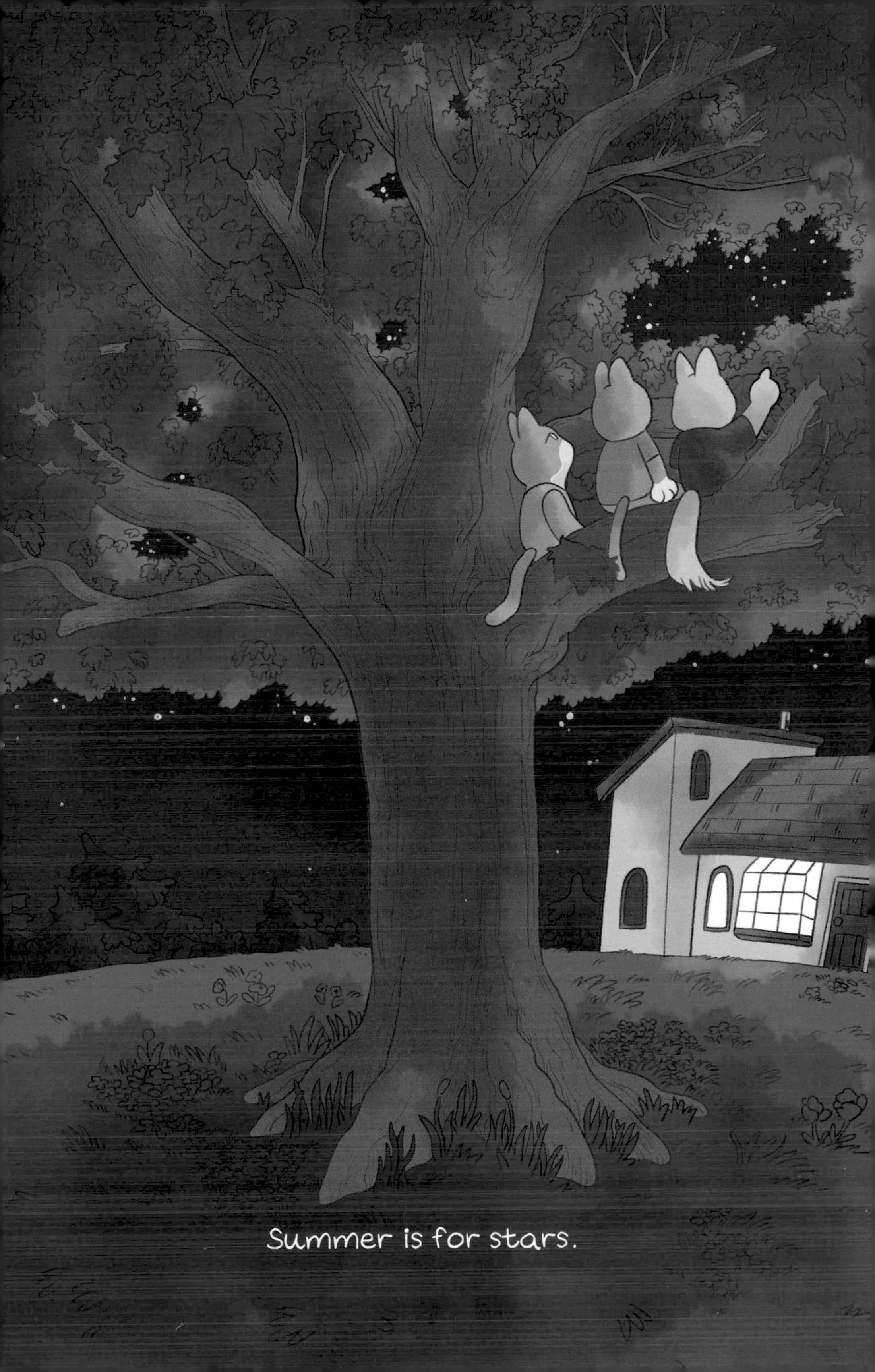

Summer is for stars.

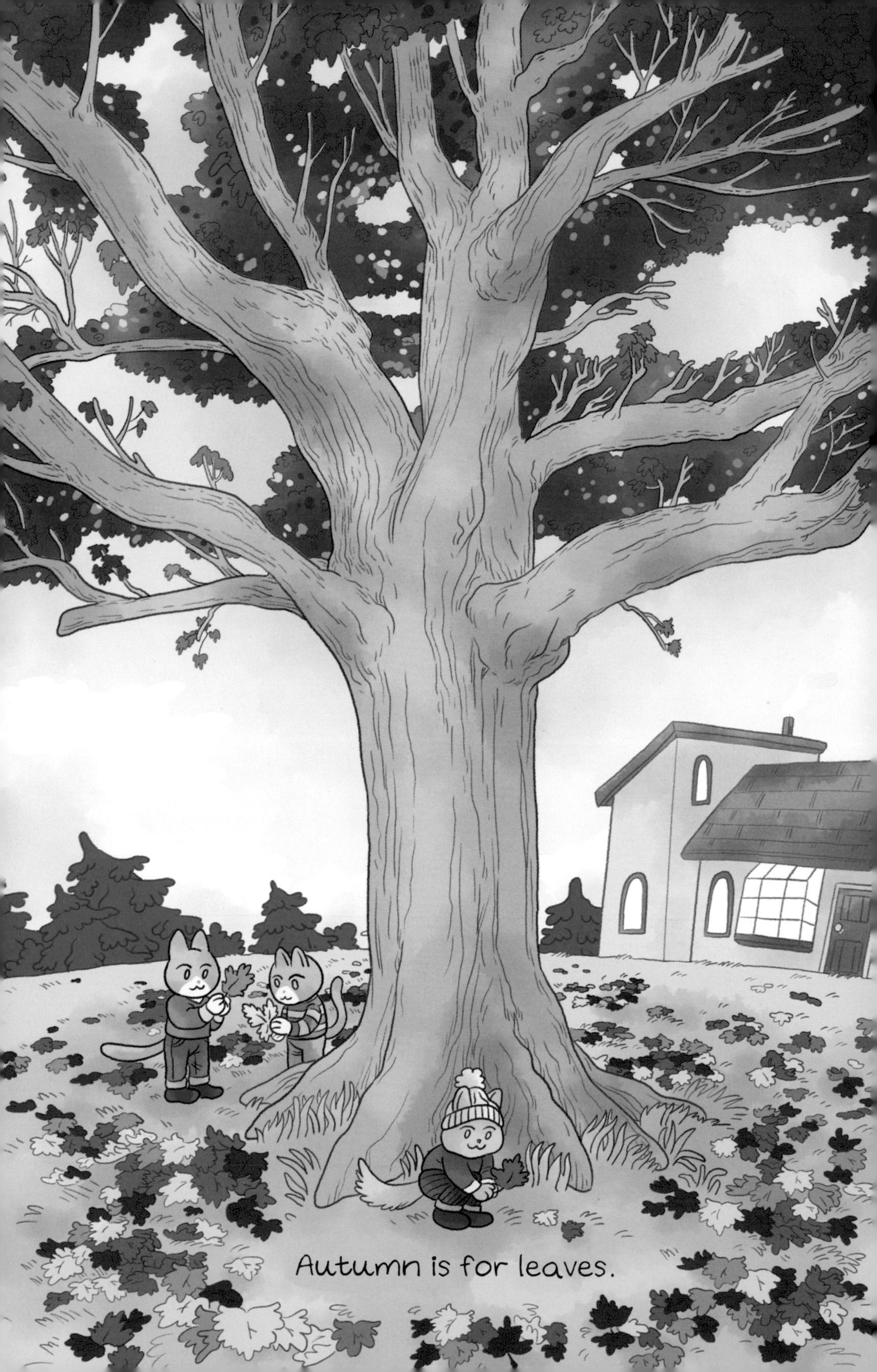

Autumn is for leaves.

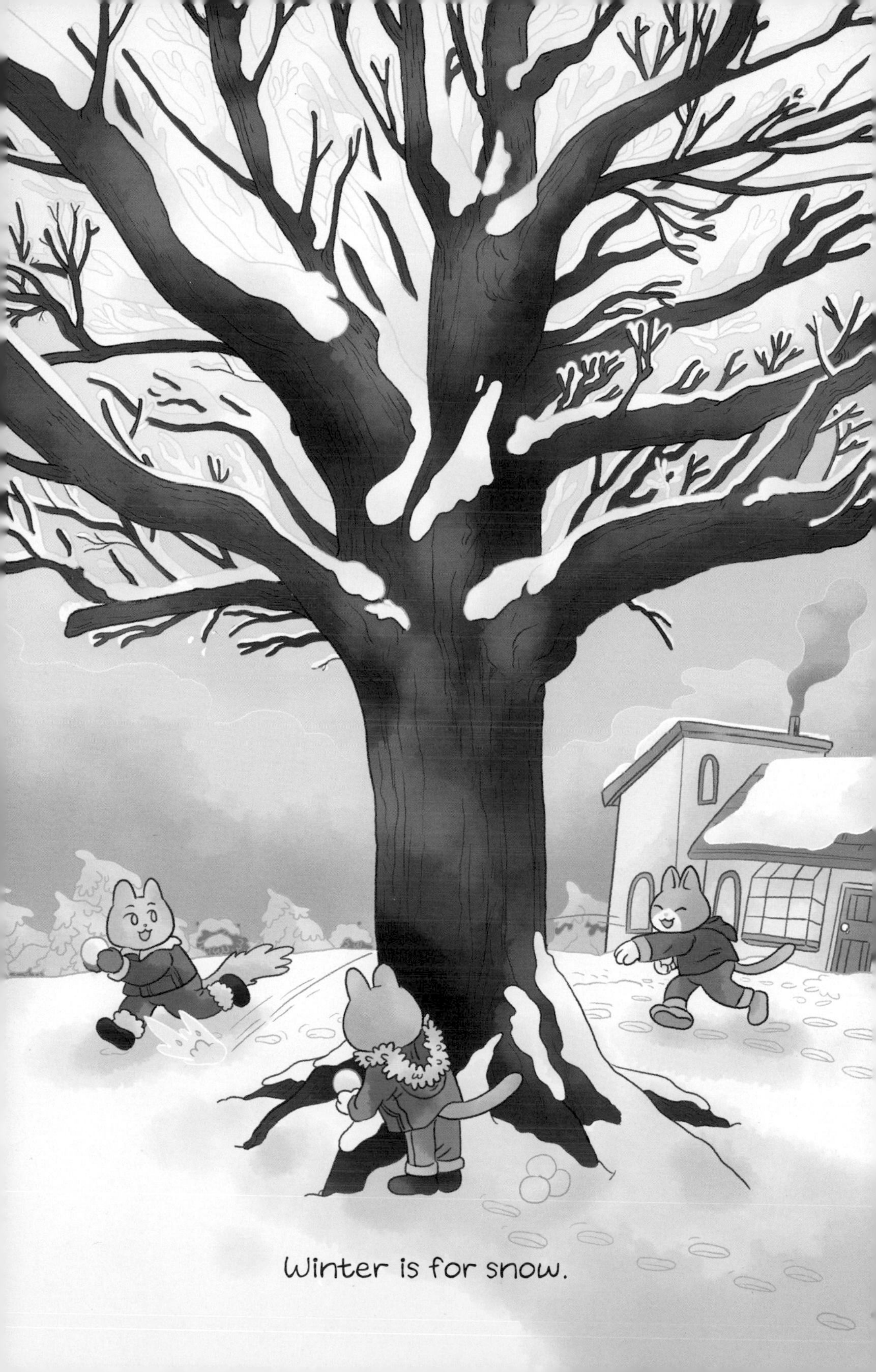

Winter is for snow.

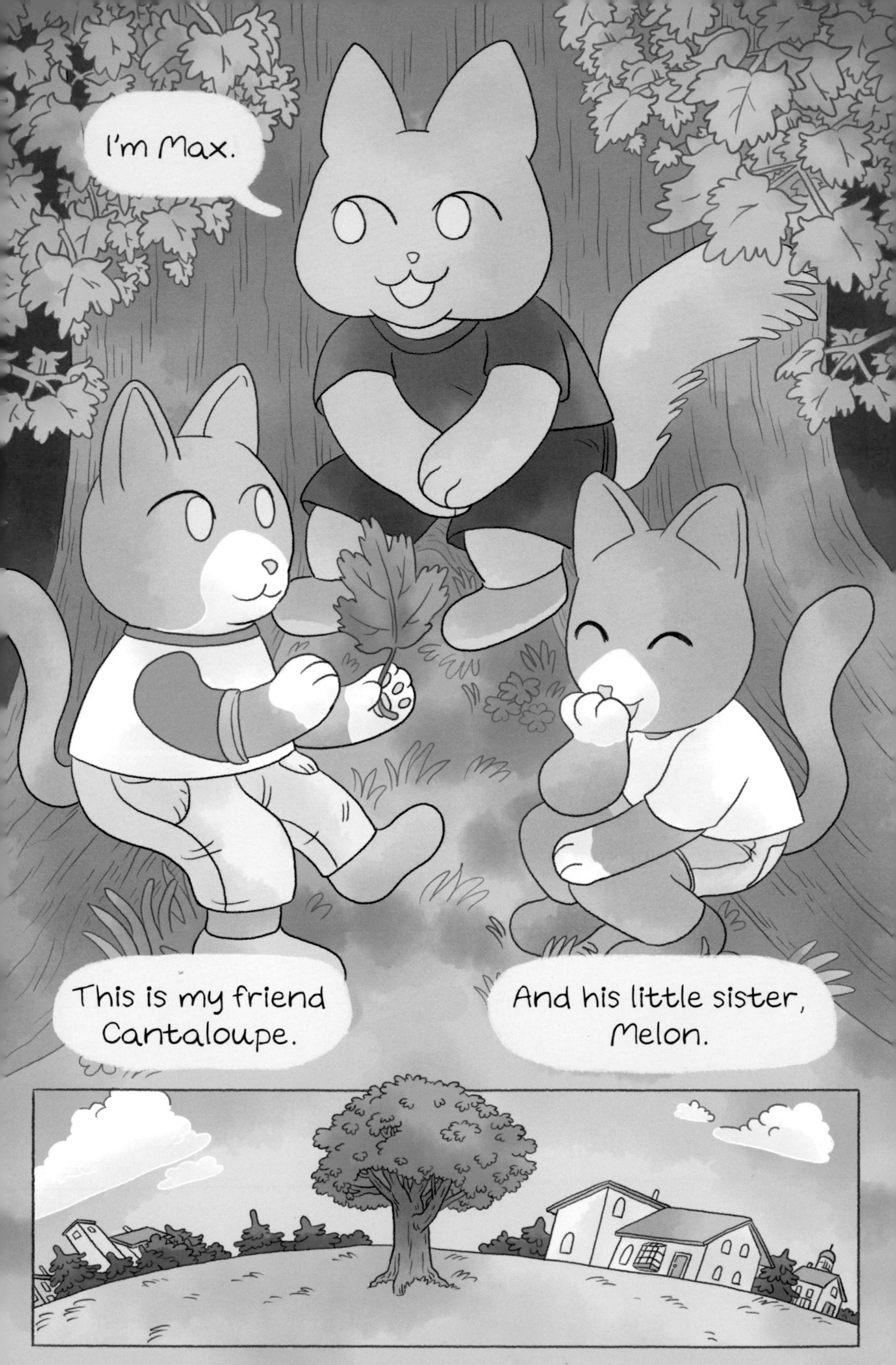
I'm Max.
This is my friend Cantaloupe.
And his little sister, Melon.

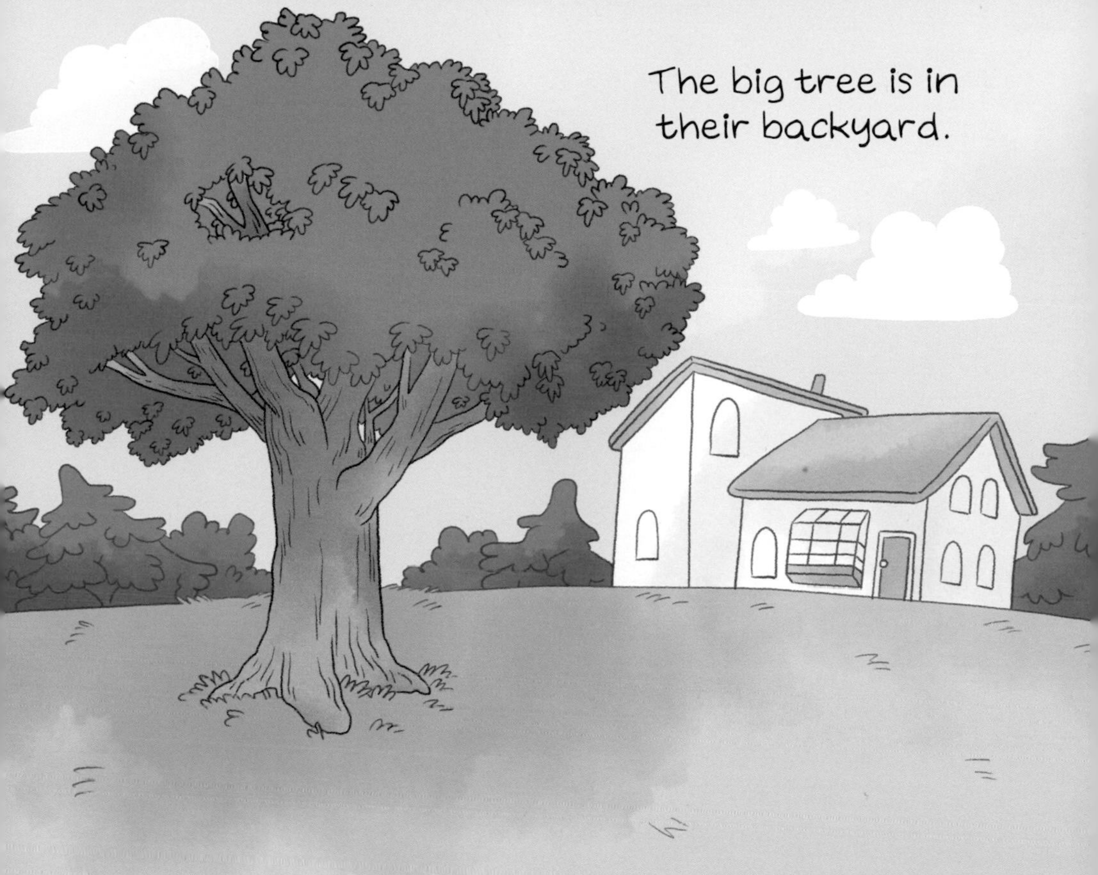
The big tree is in their backyard.

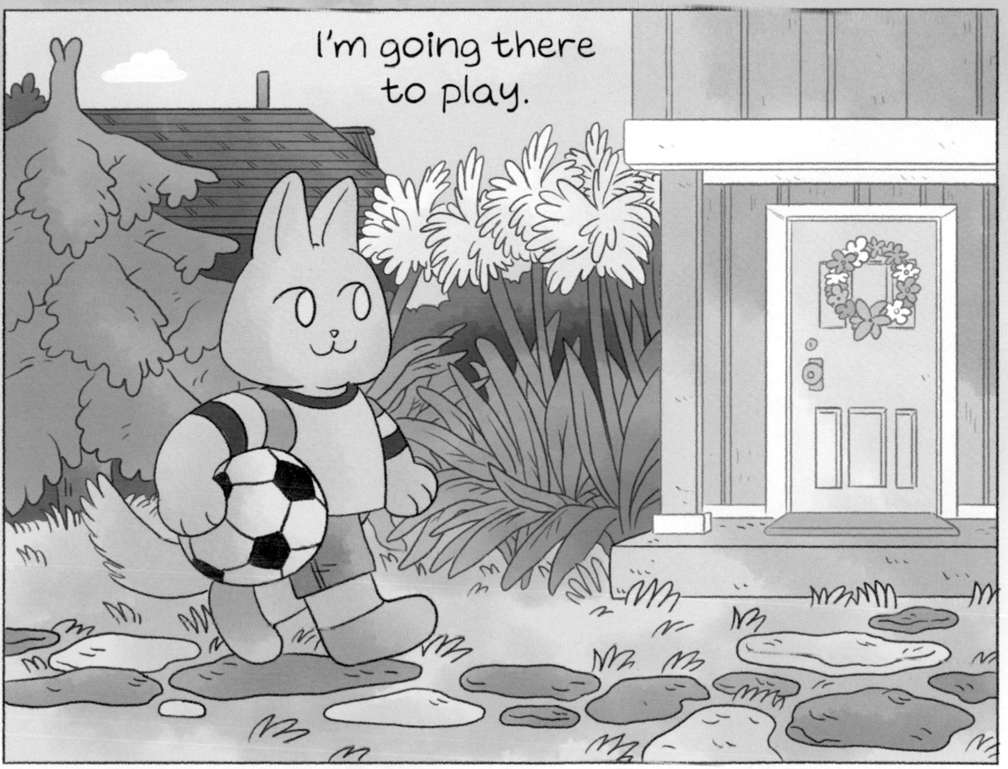
I'm going there to play.

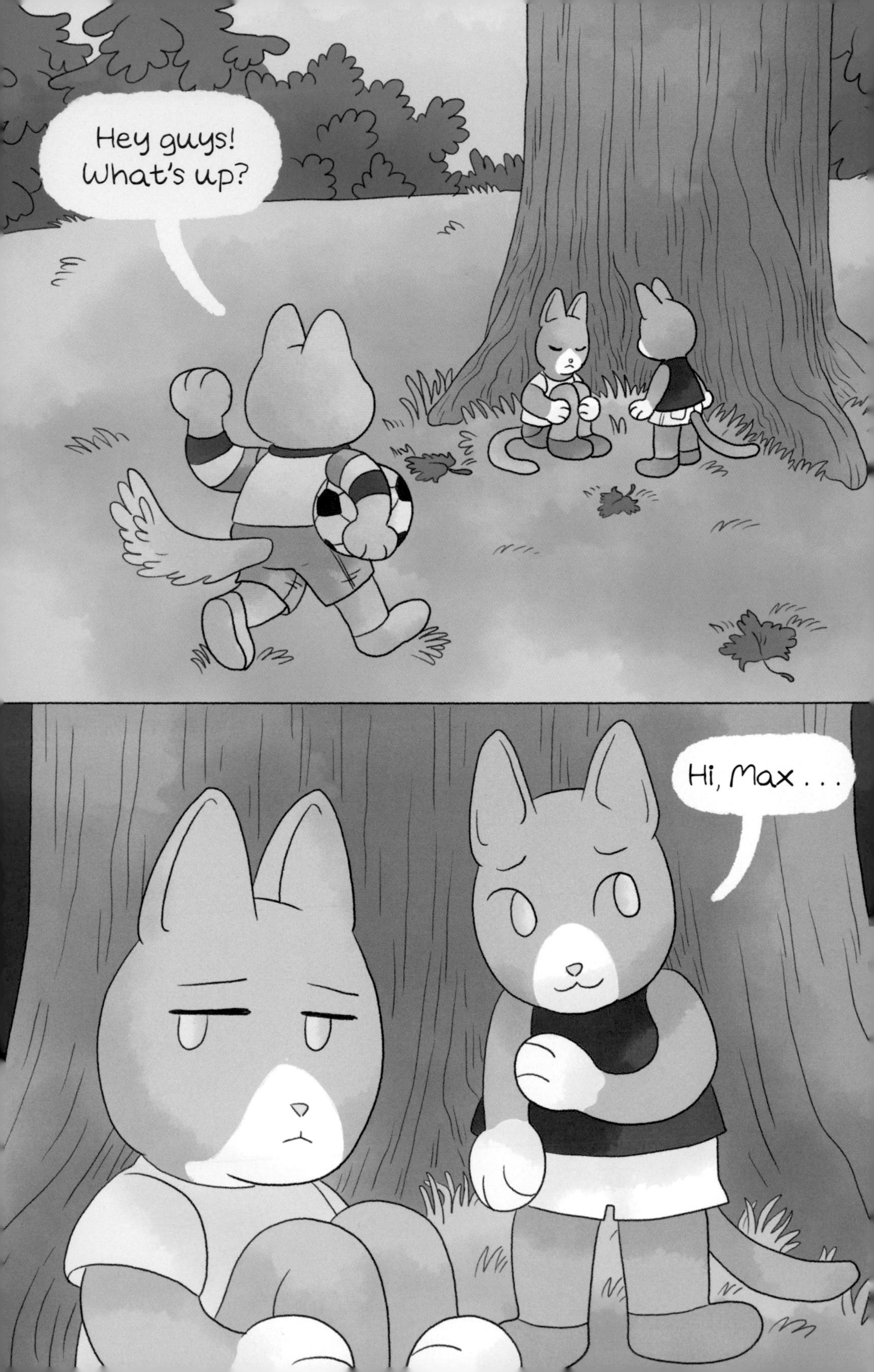
Hey guys! What's up?
Hi, Max . . .

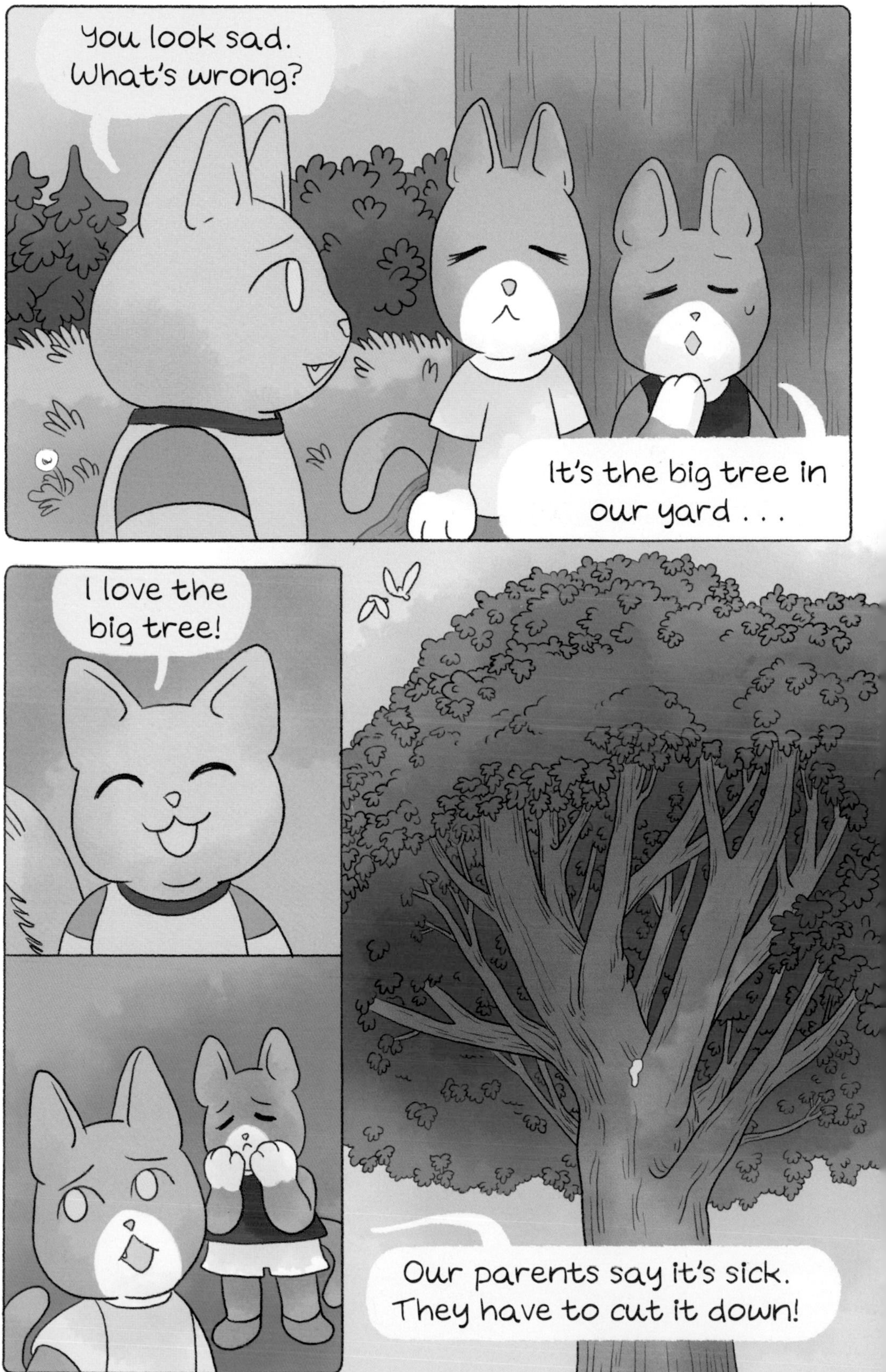
You look sad. What's wrong?
It's the big tree in our yard . . .
I love the big tree!
Our parents say it's sick. They have to cut it down!

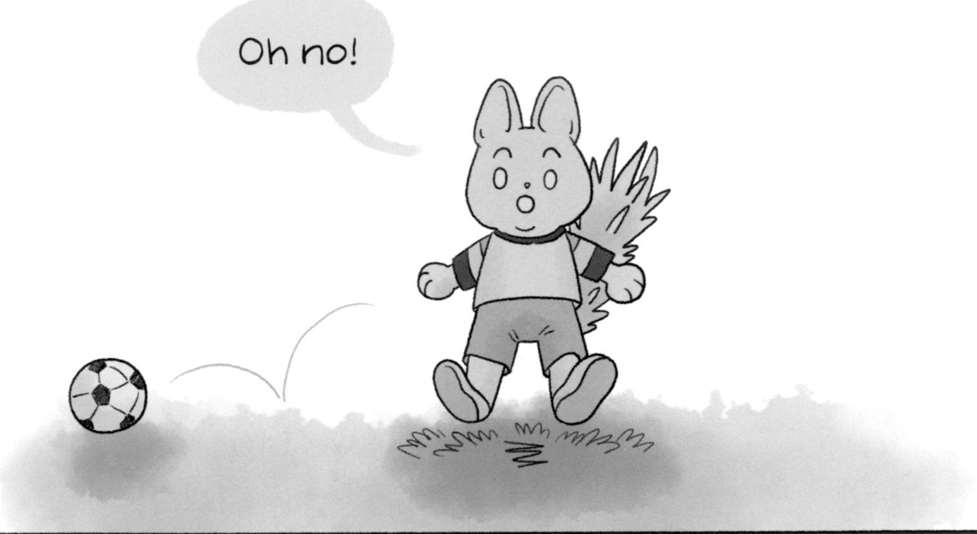
Oh no!

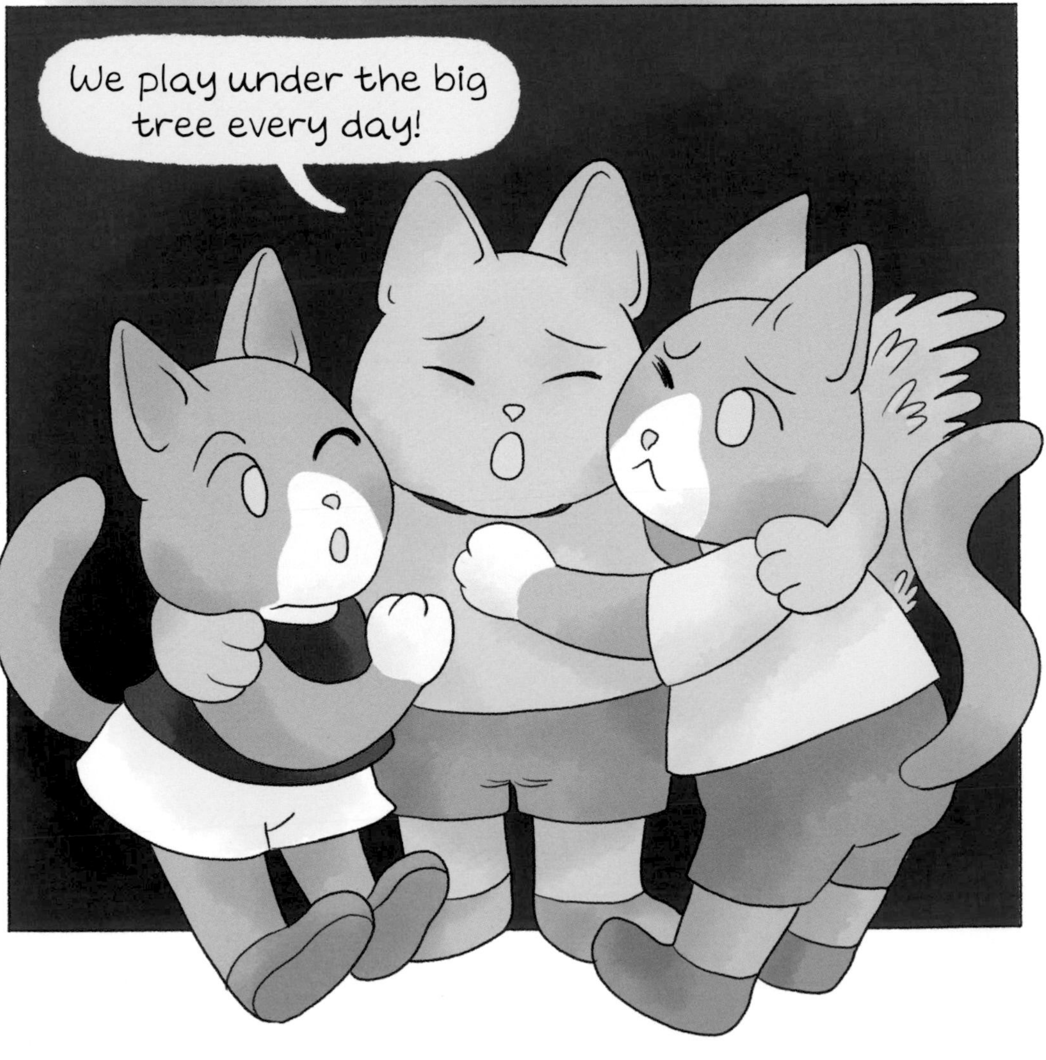
We play under the big tree every day!

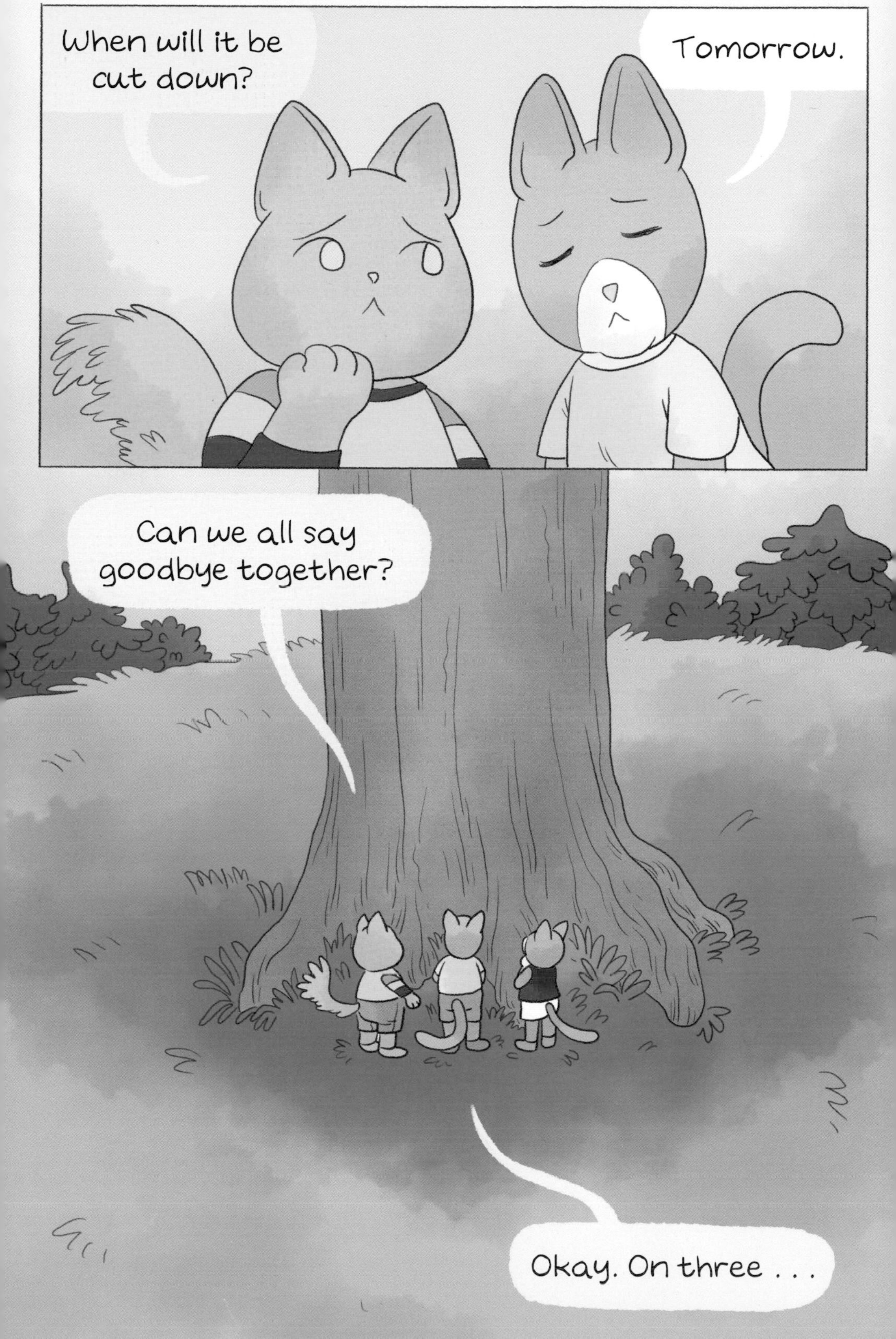
When will it be cut down?
Tomorrow.
Can we all say goodbye together?
Okay. On three . . .

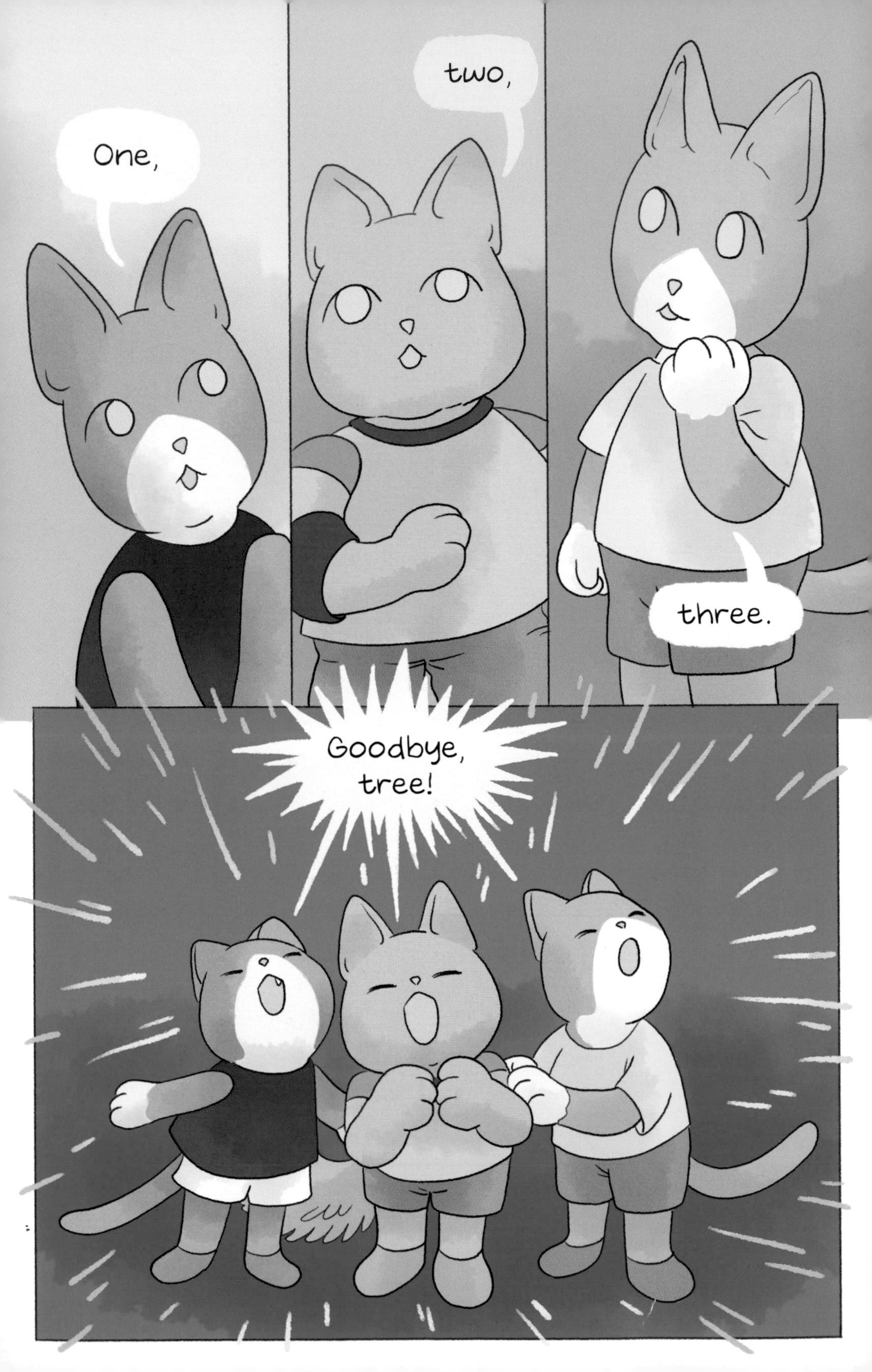
One,
two,
three.
Goodbye, tree!

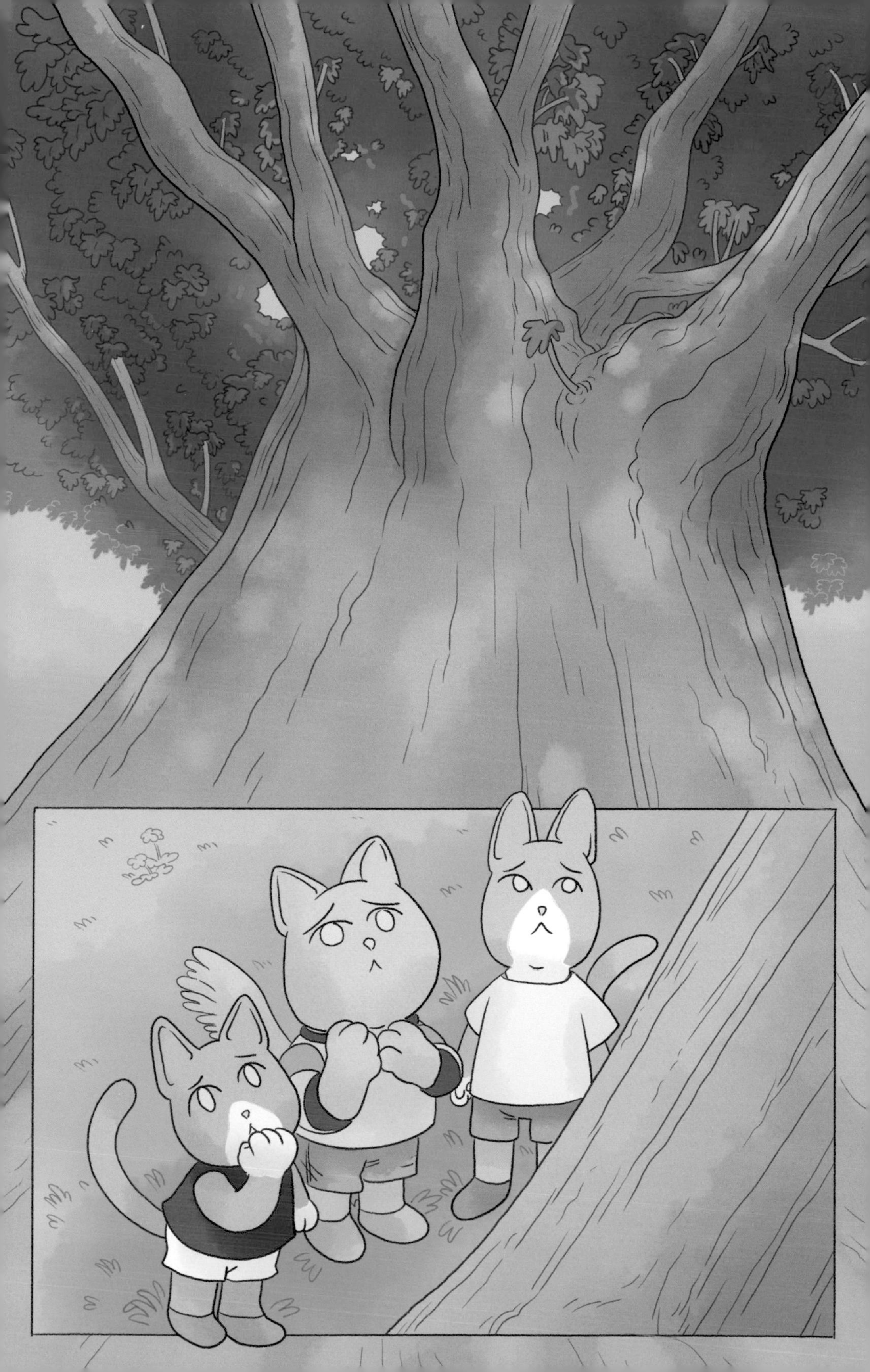

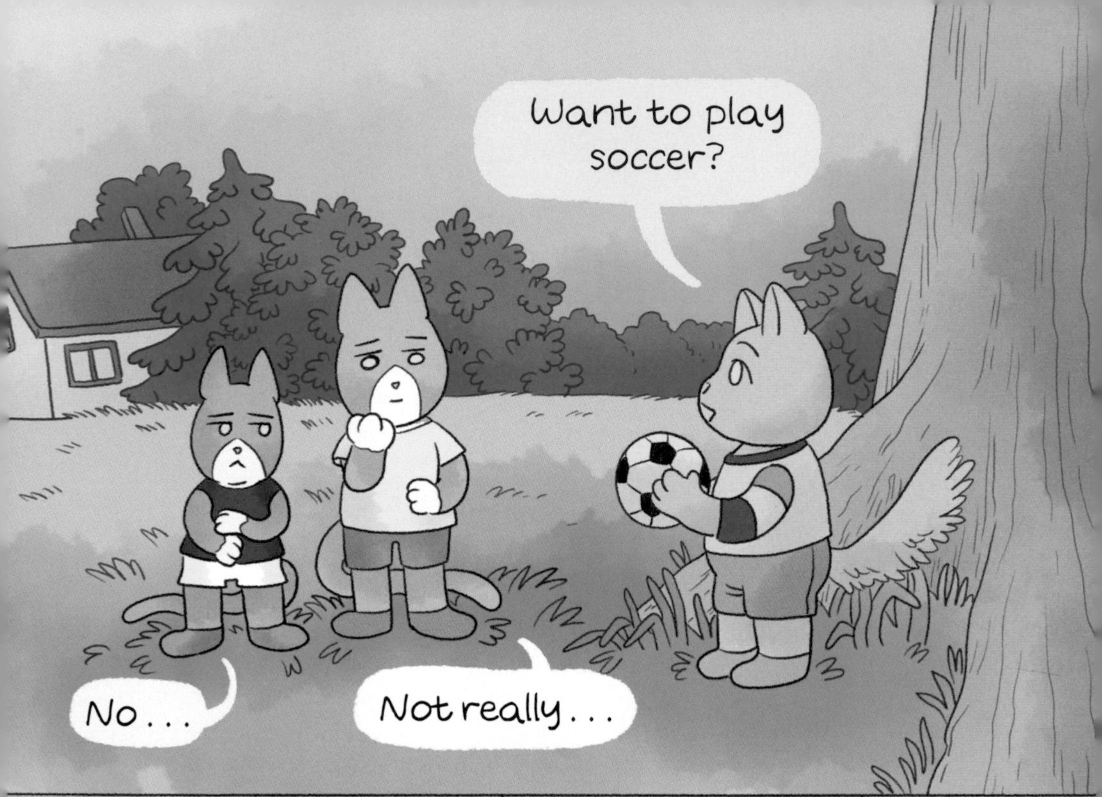
Want to play soccer?
No...
Not really...

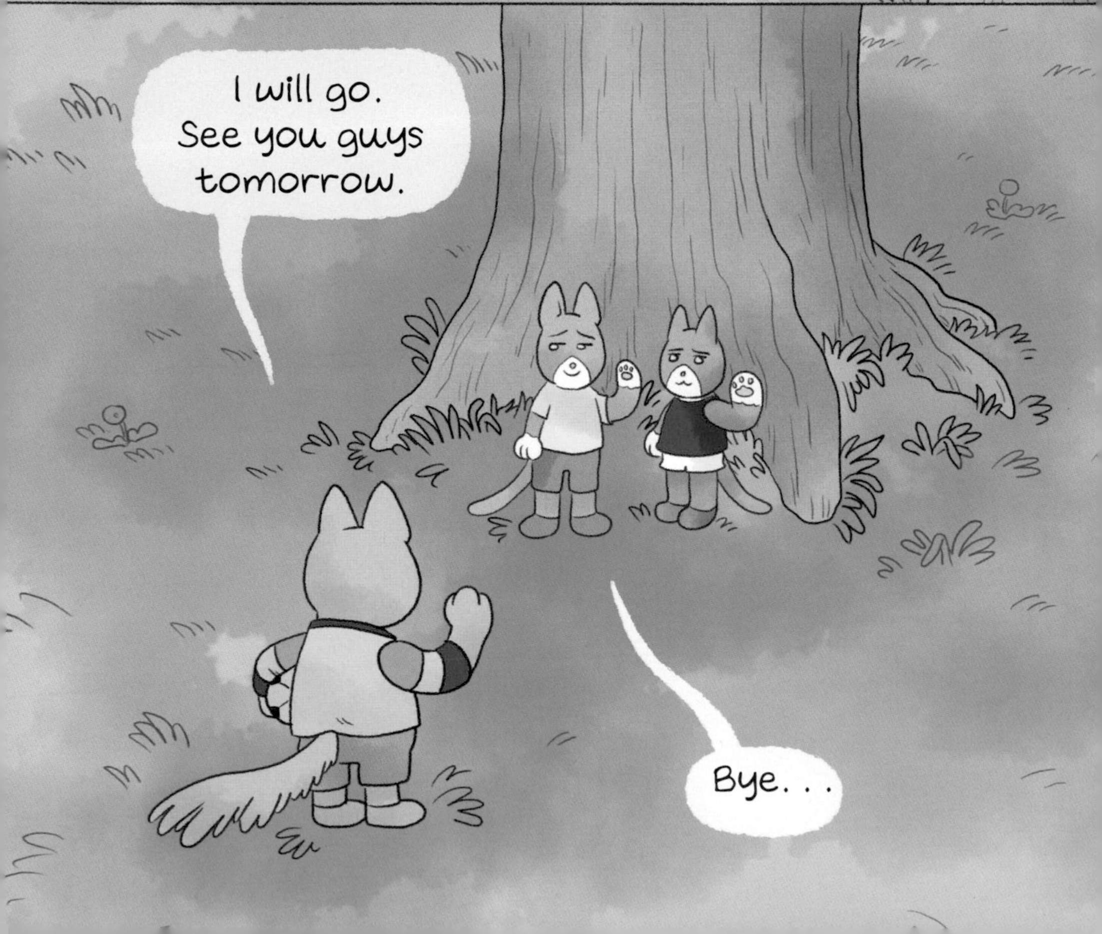
I will go. See you guys tomorrow.
Bye...

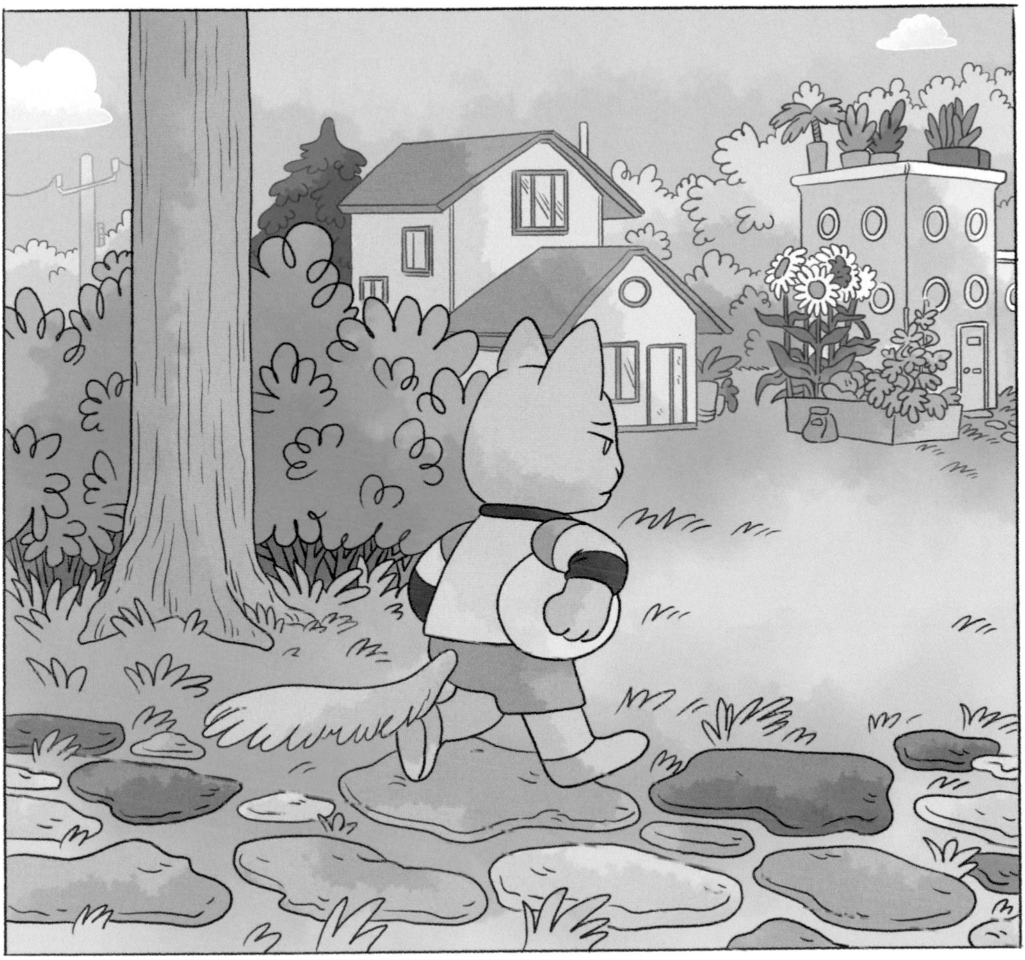

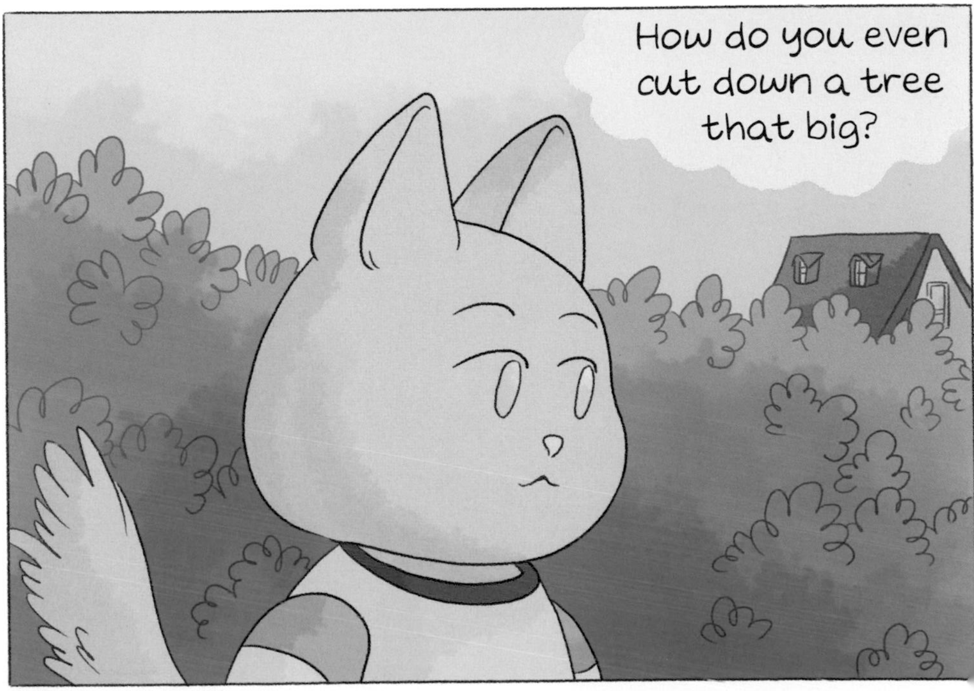
How do you even cut down a tree that big?

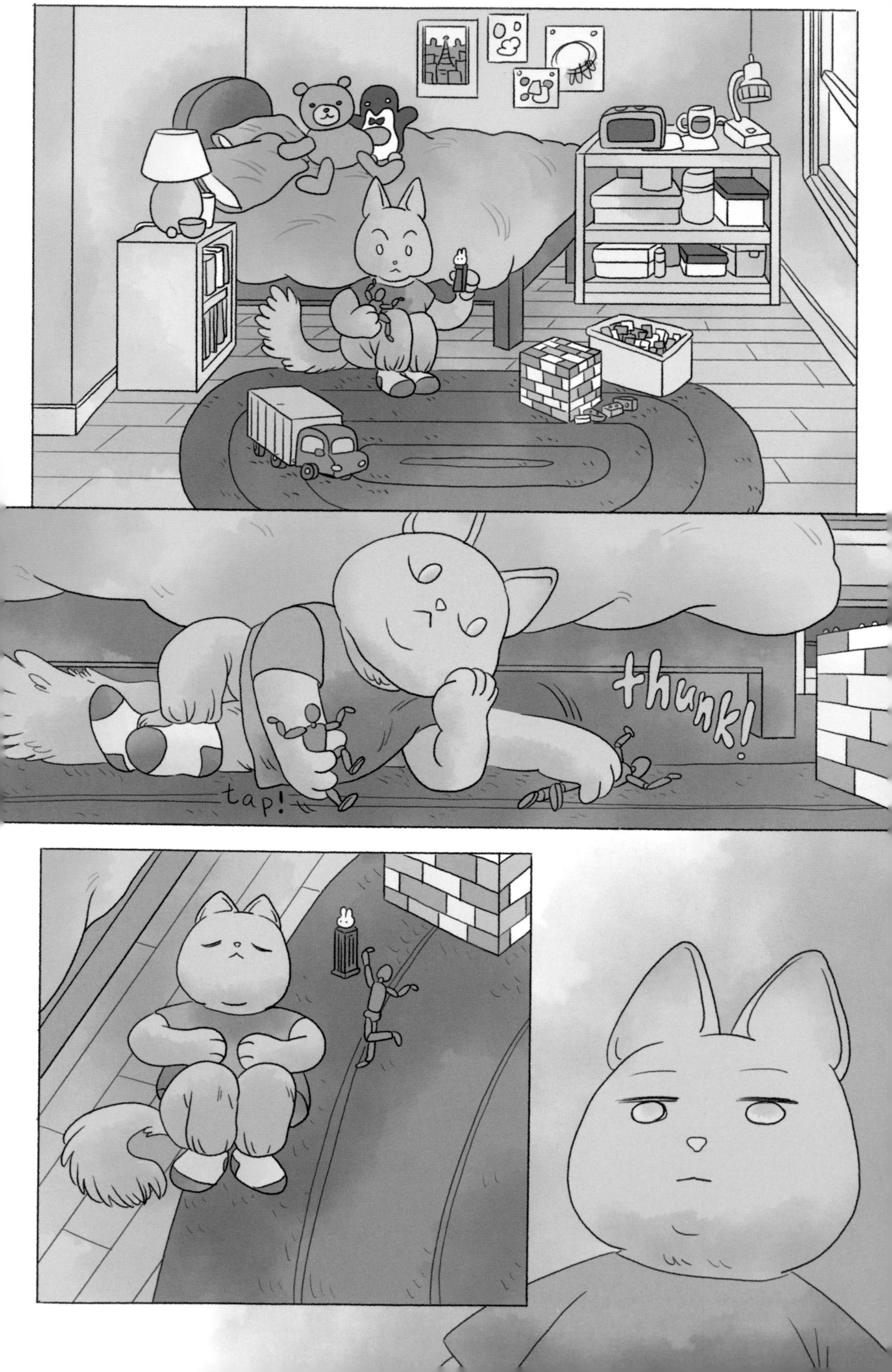
thunk!
tap!

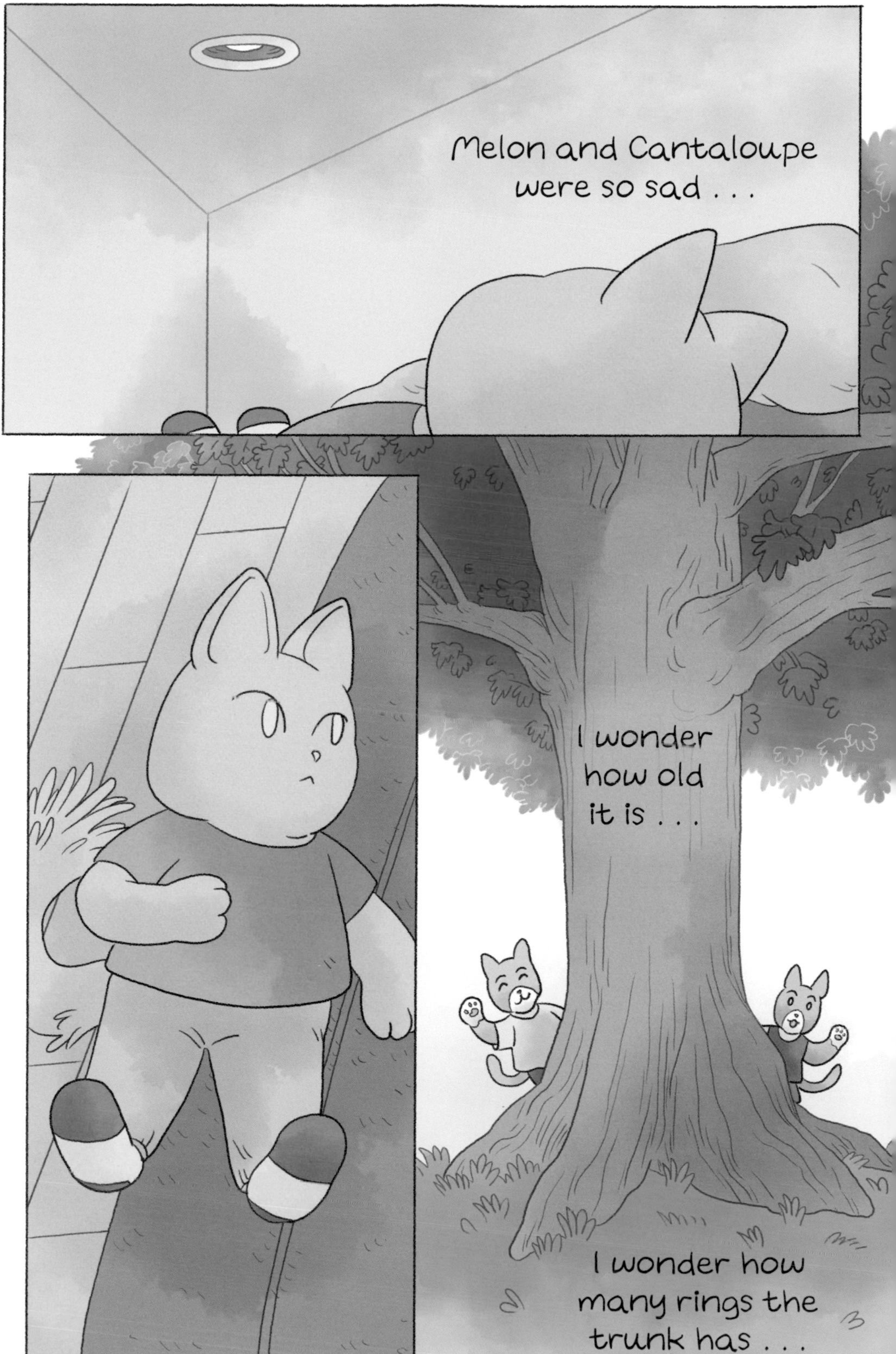
Melon and Cantaloupe were so sad . . .
I wonder how old it is . . .
I wonder how many rings the trunk has . . .

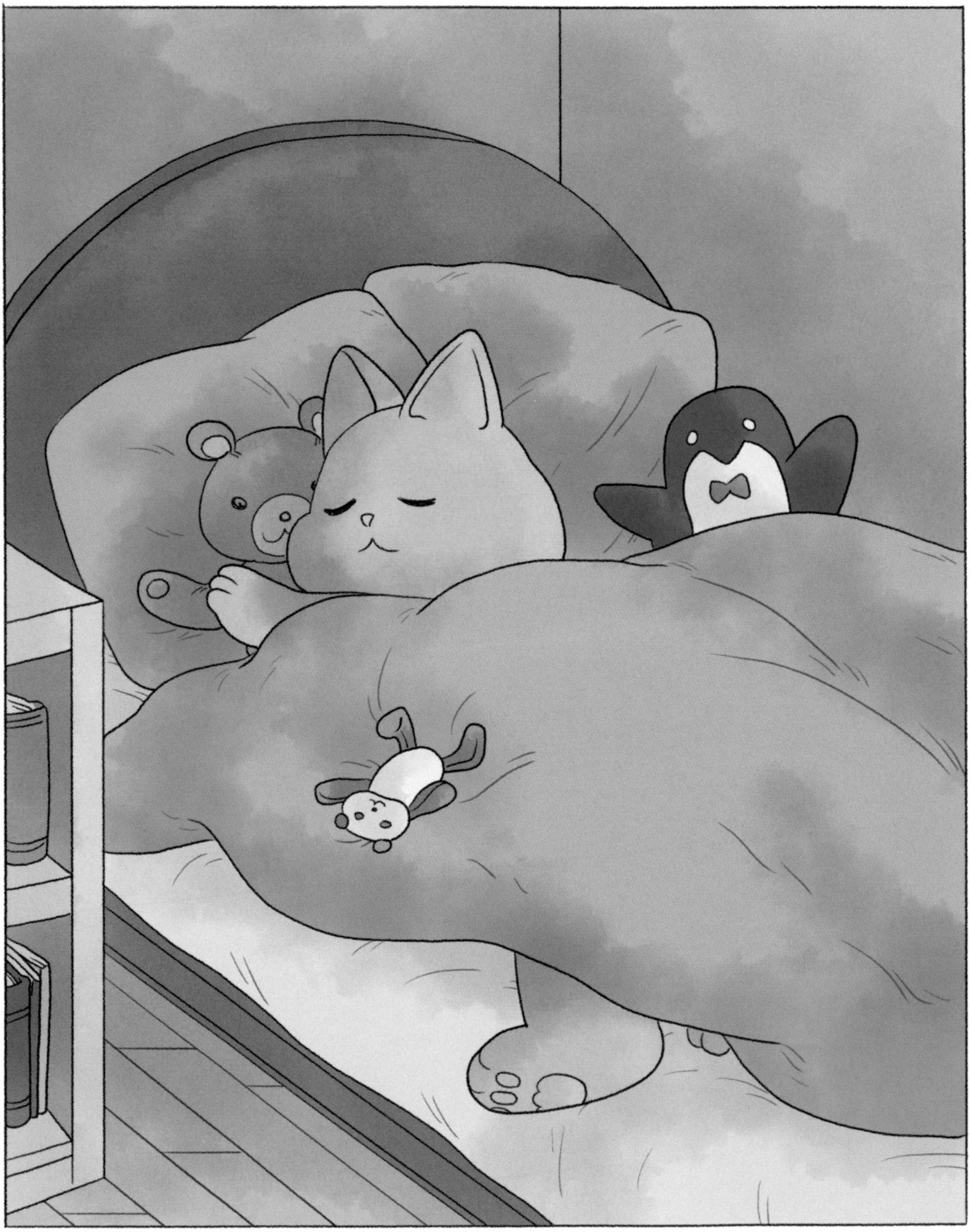

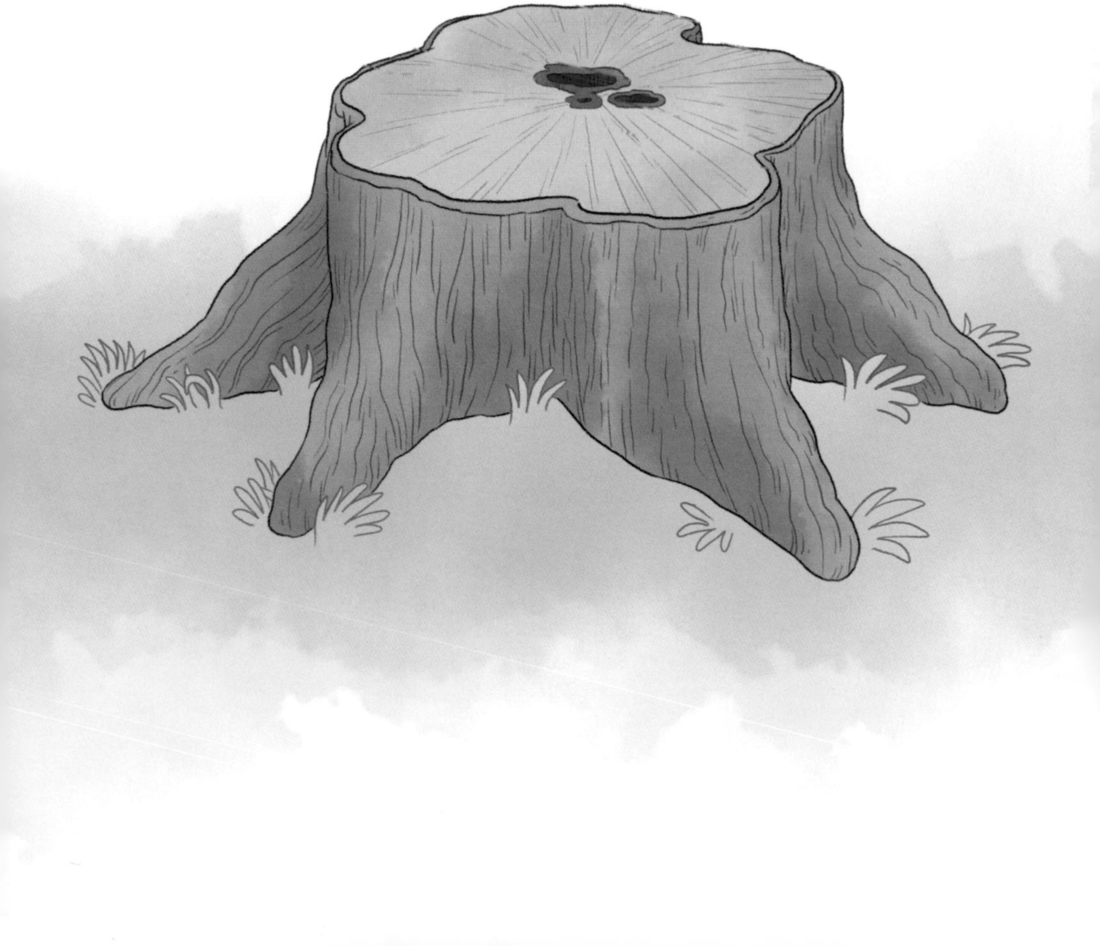

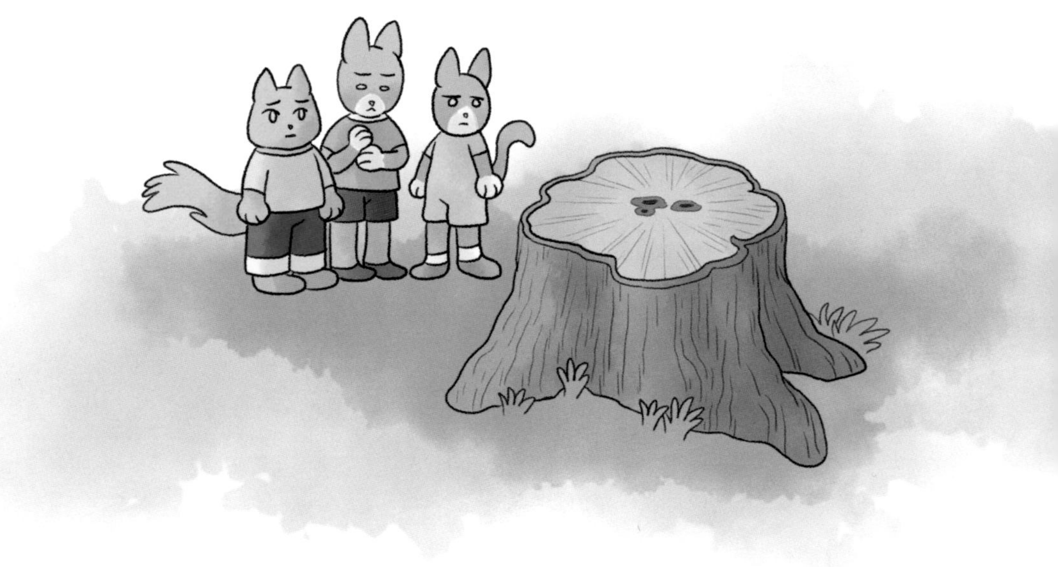

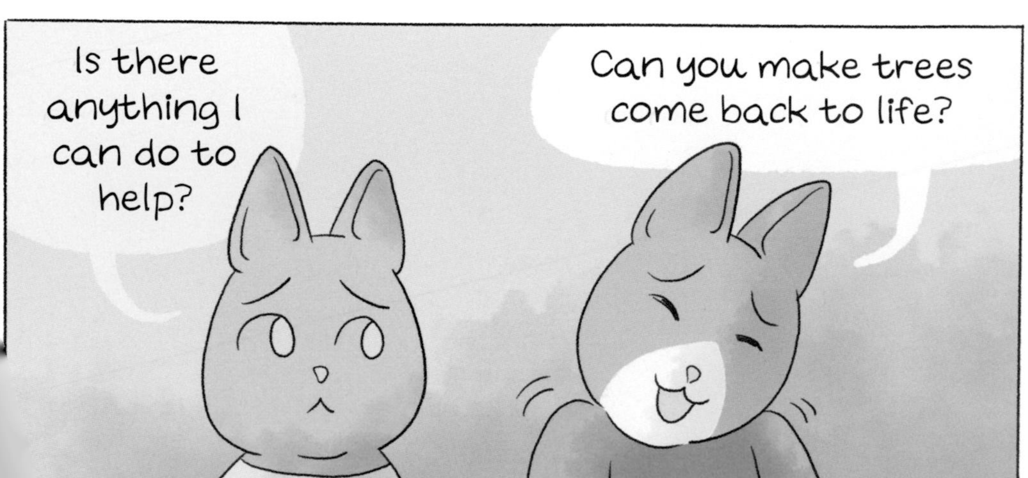
Is there anything I can do to help?
Can you make trees come back to life?

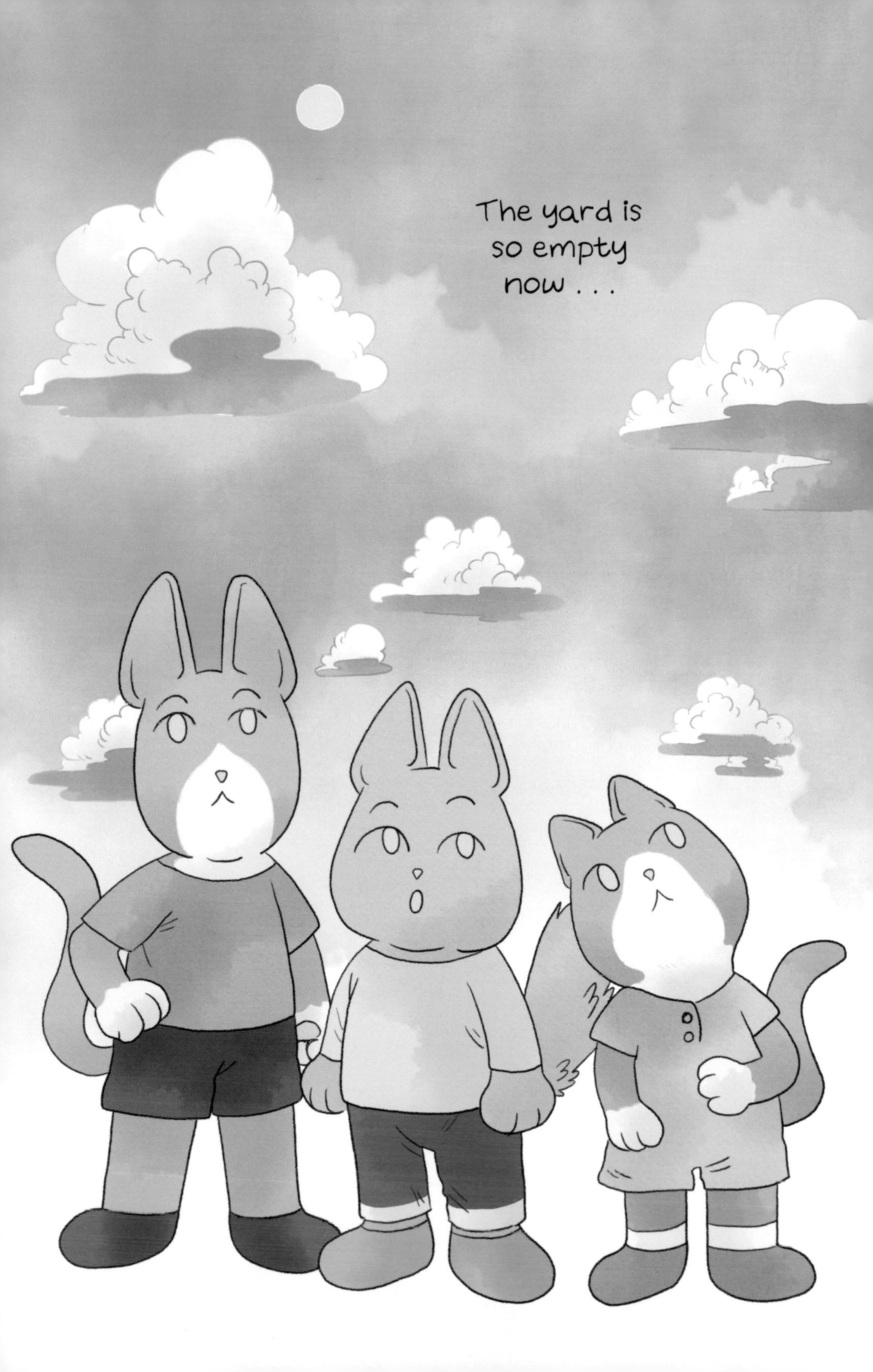
The yard is
so empty
now . . .

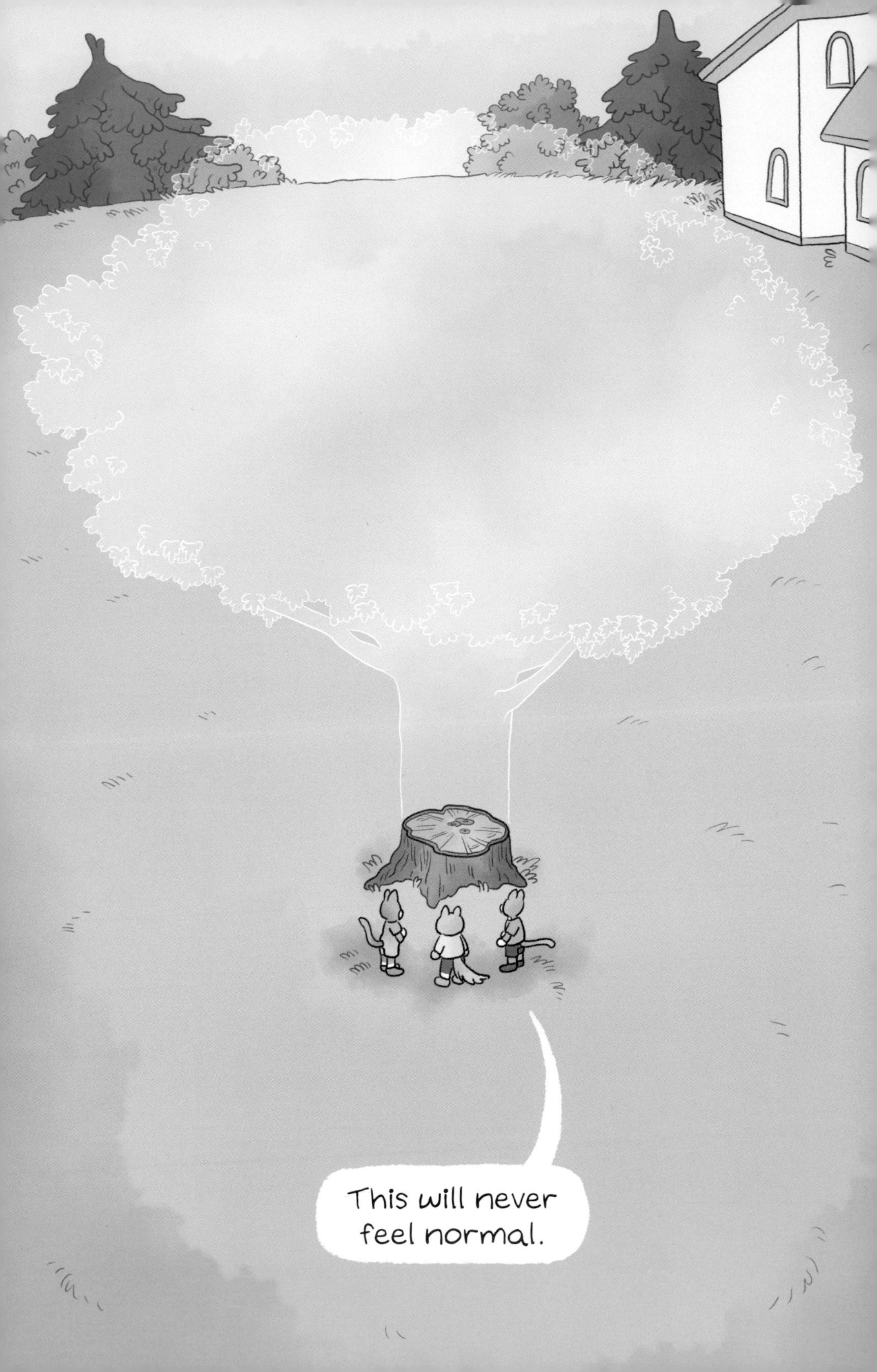
This will never feel normal.

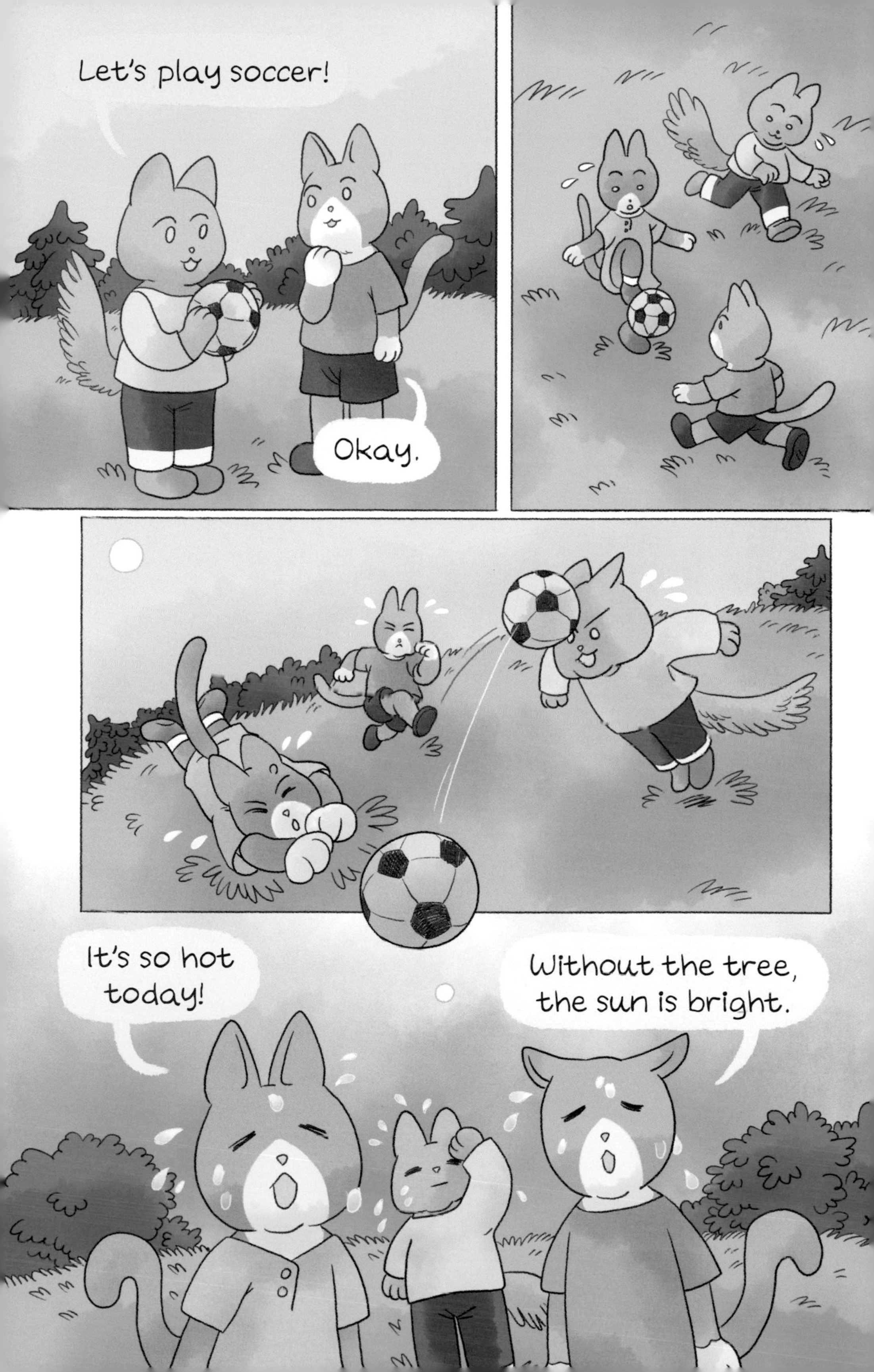
Let's play soccer!
Okay.
It's so hot today!
Without the tree, the sun is bright.

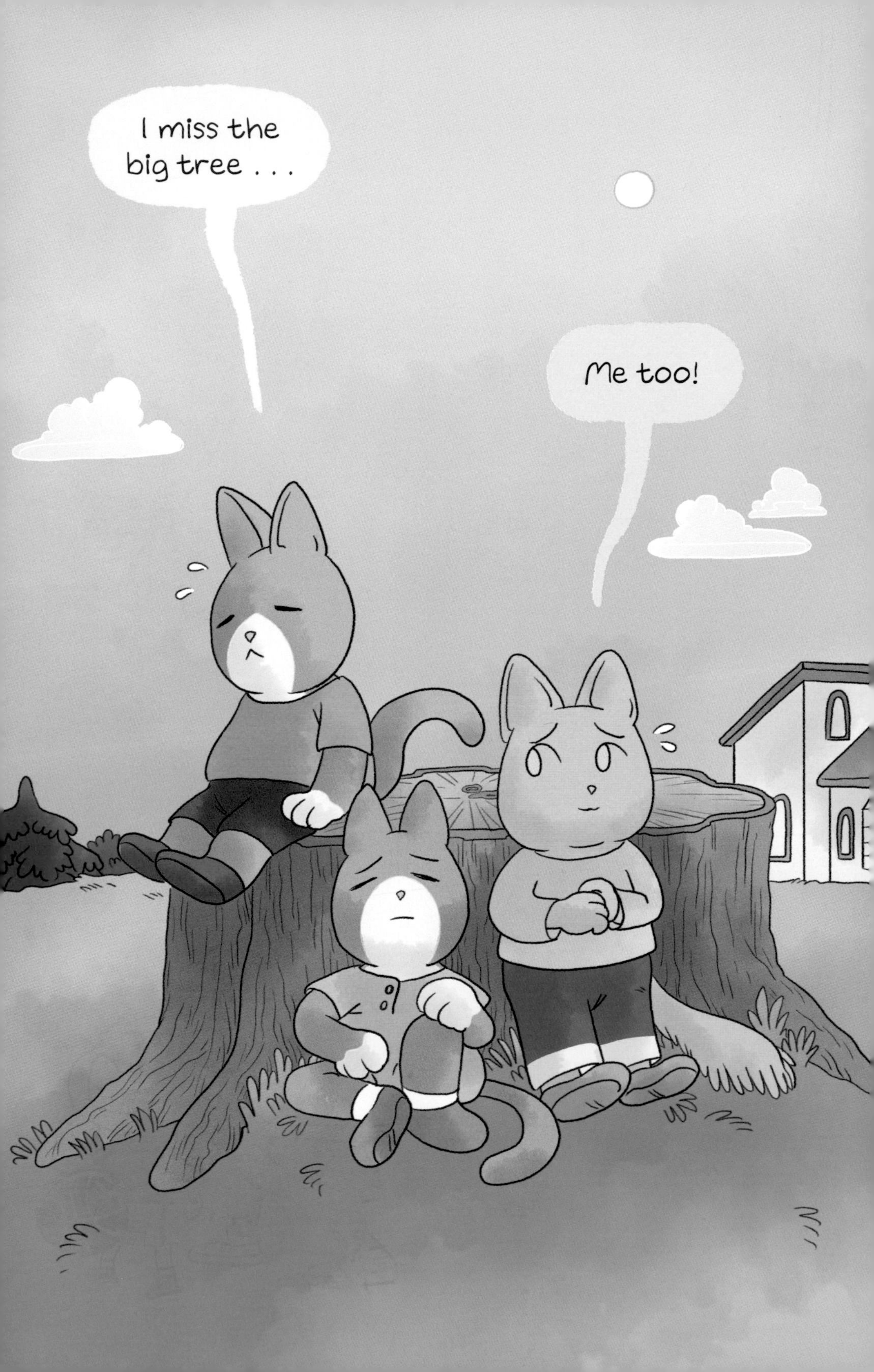
I miss the big tree . . .
Me too!

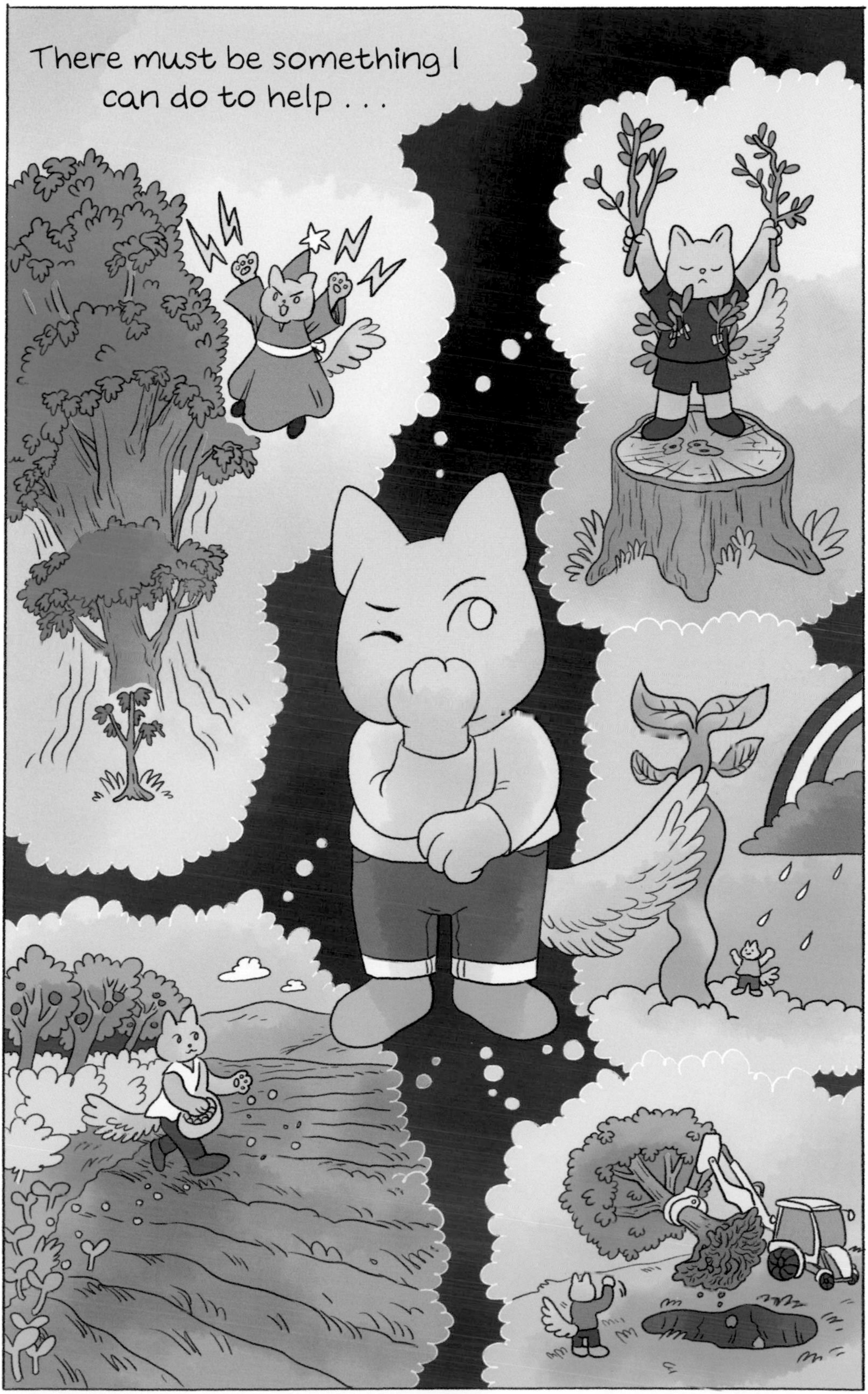
There must be something I can do to help . . .

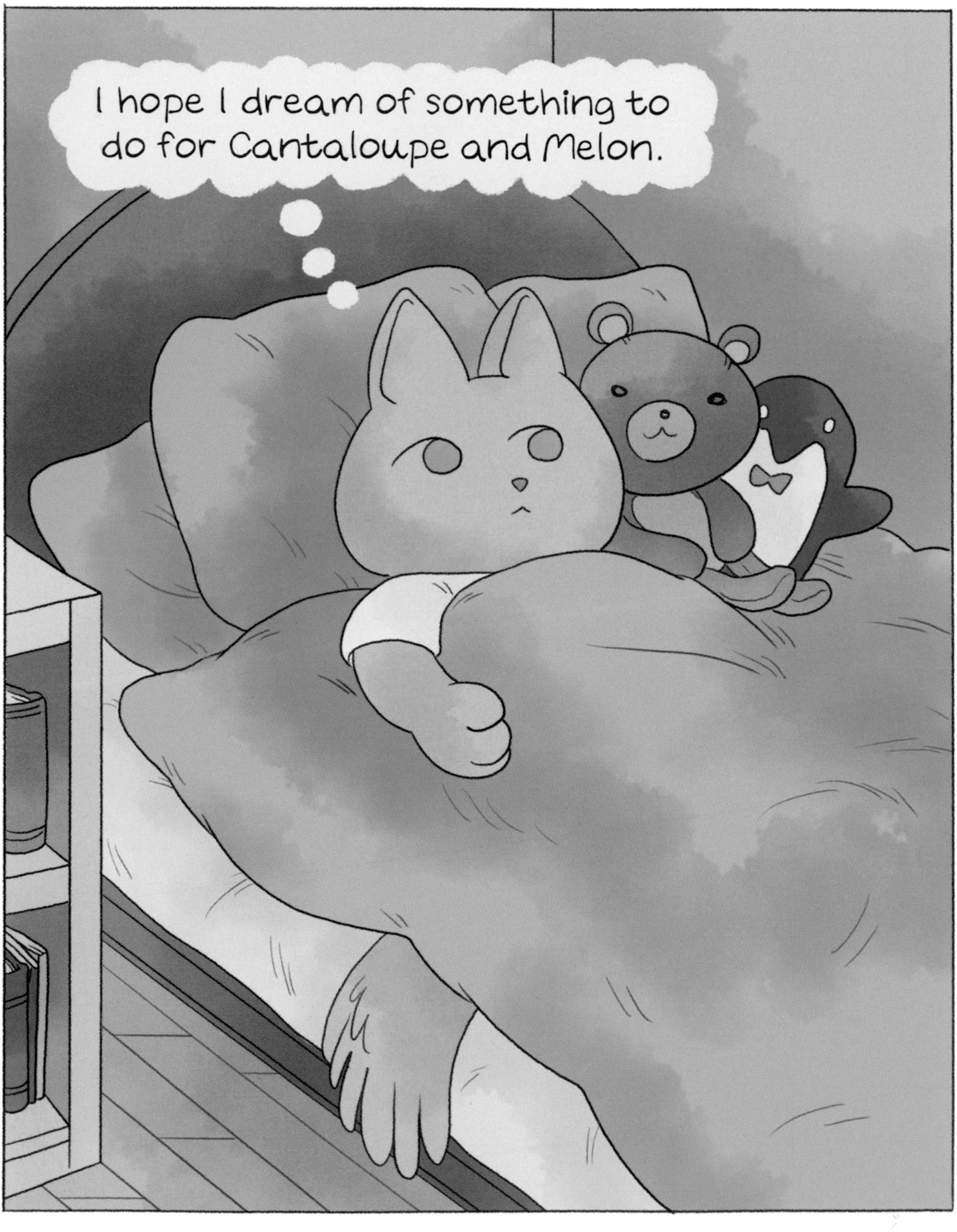
I hope I dream of something to do for Cantaloupe and Melon.

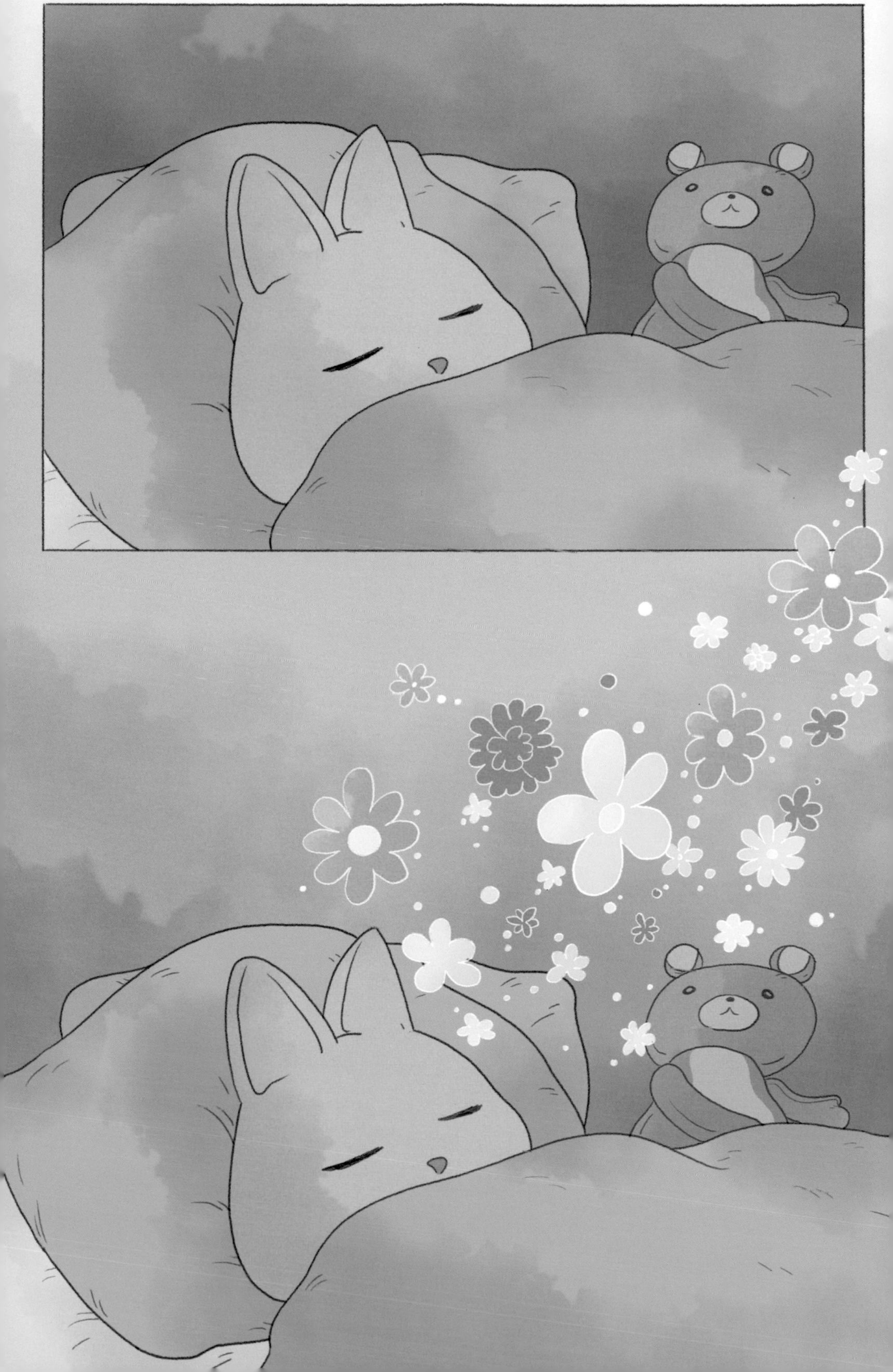

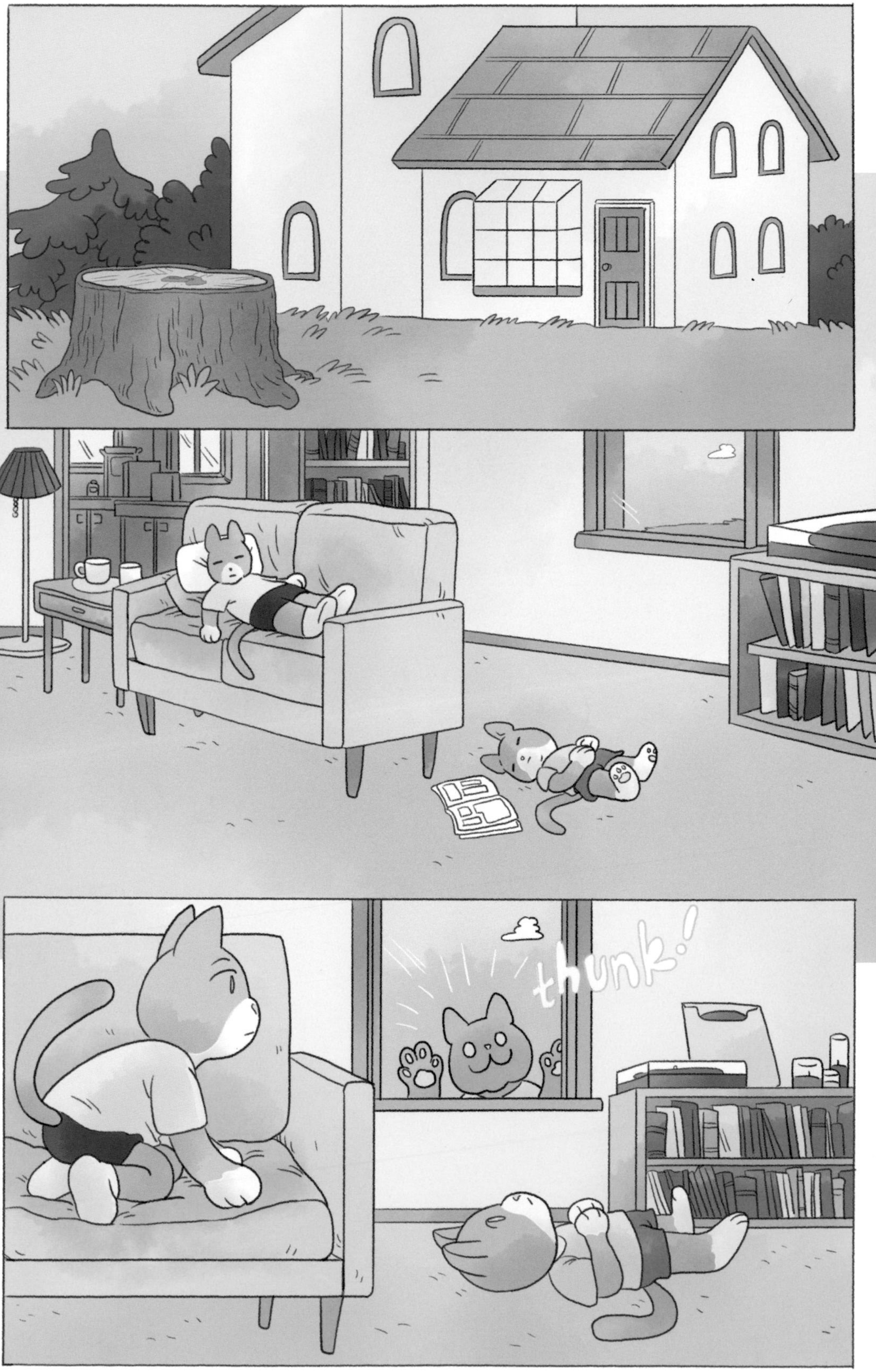
thunk!

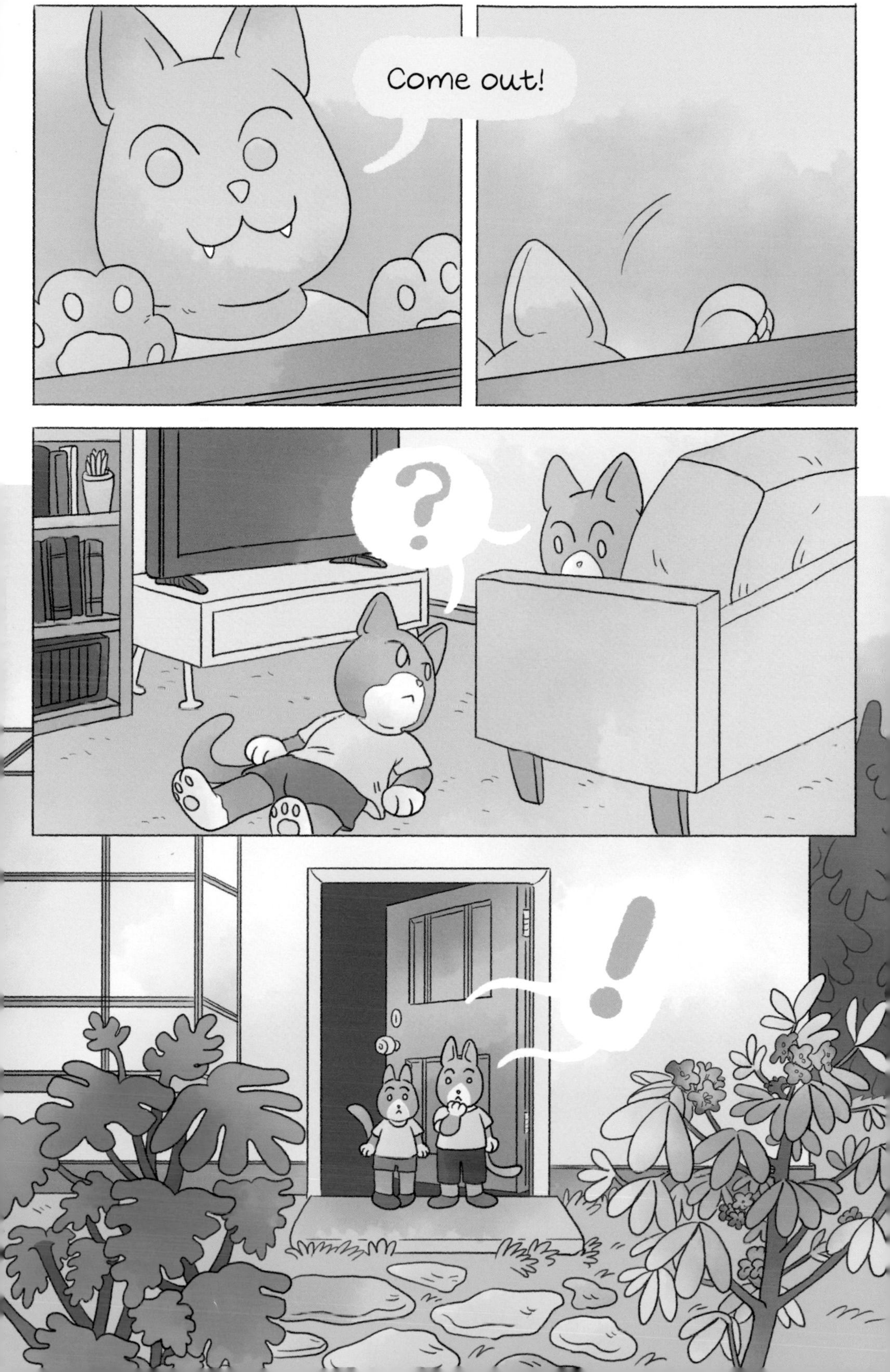
Come out!
?
!

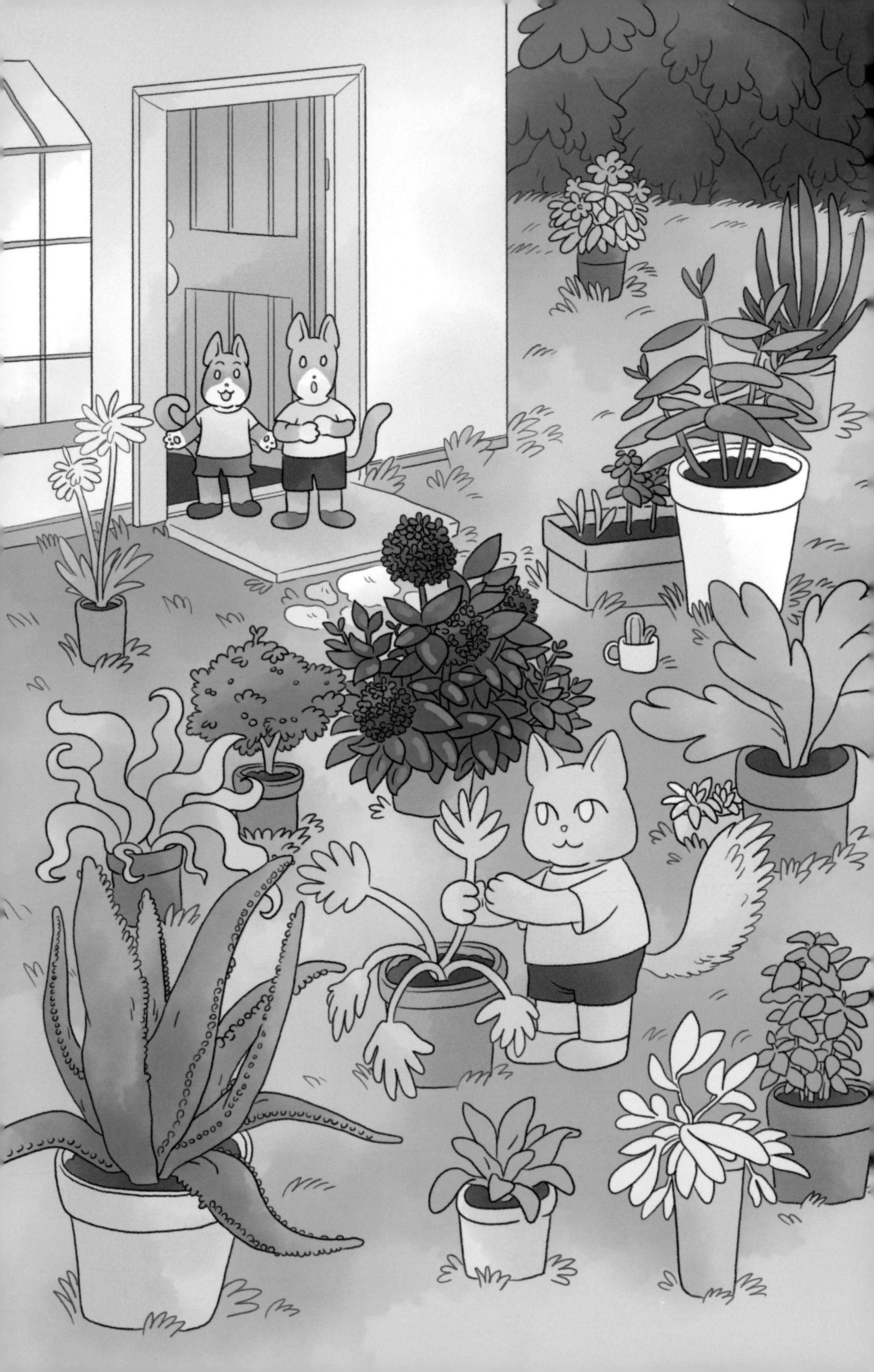

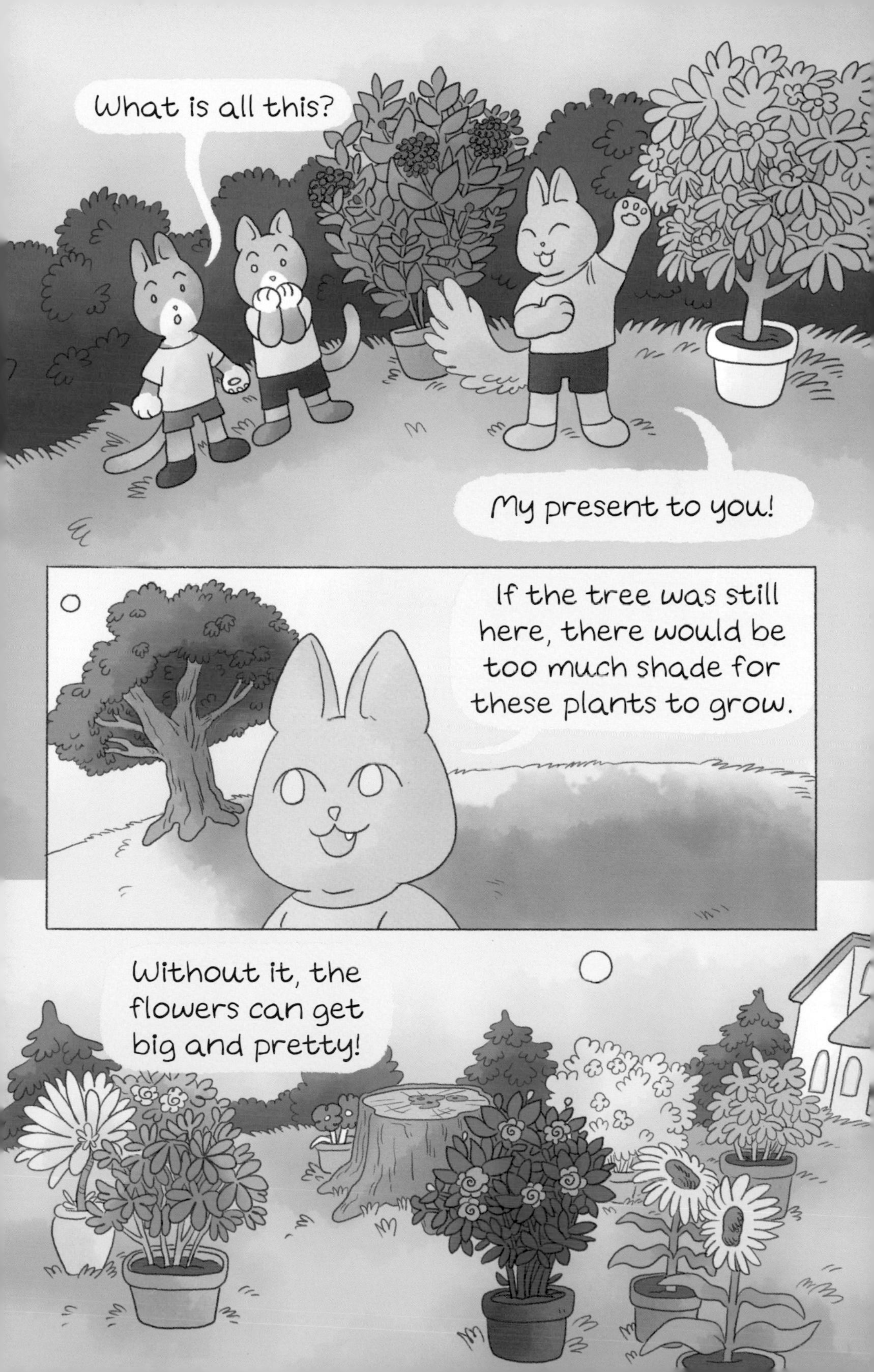
What is all this?
My present to you!
If the tree was still here, there would be too much shade for these plants to grow.
Without it, the flowers can get big and pretty!

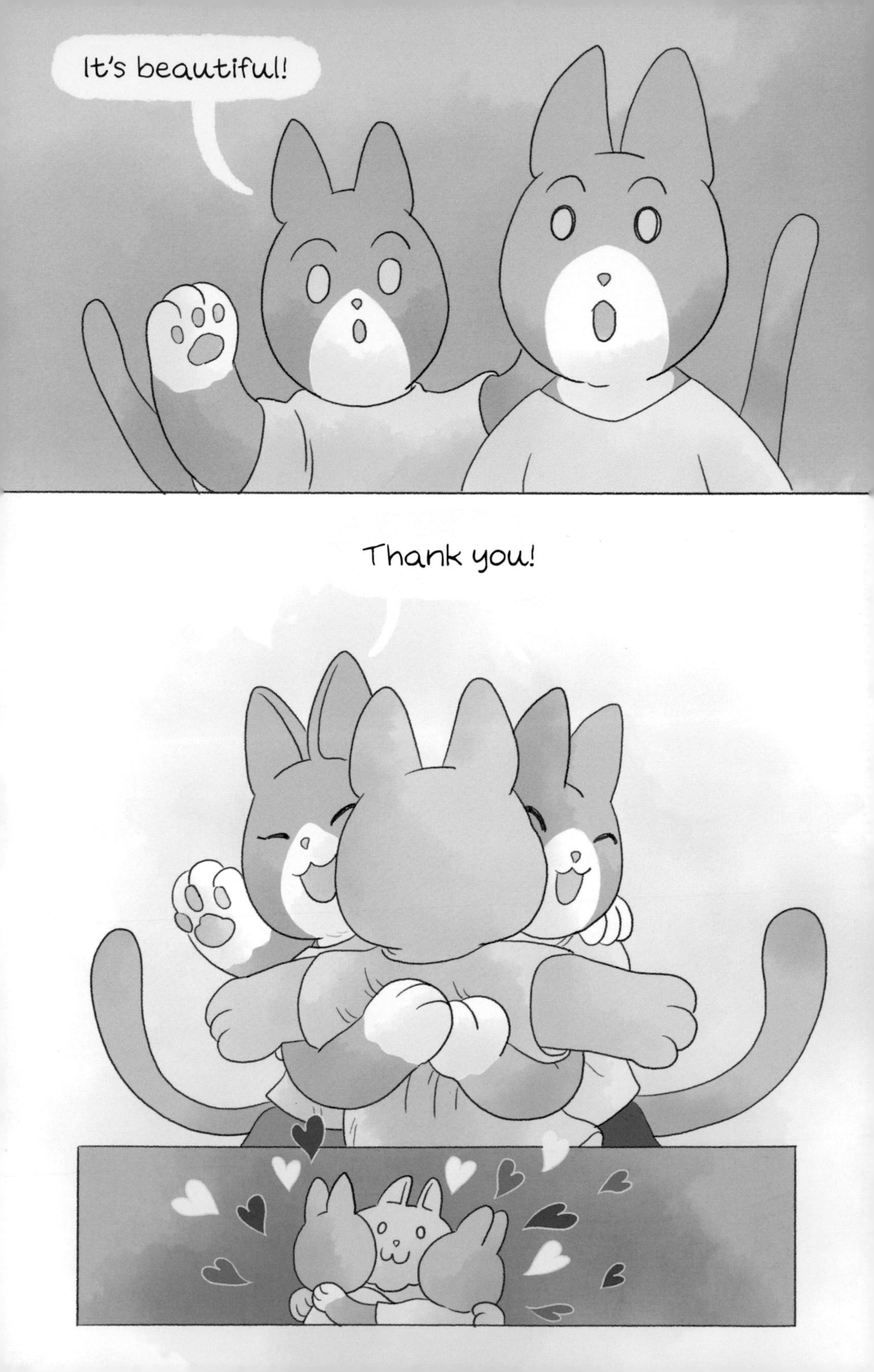
It's beautiful!
Thank you!

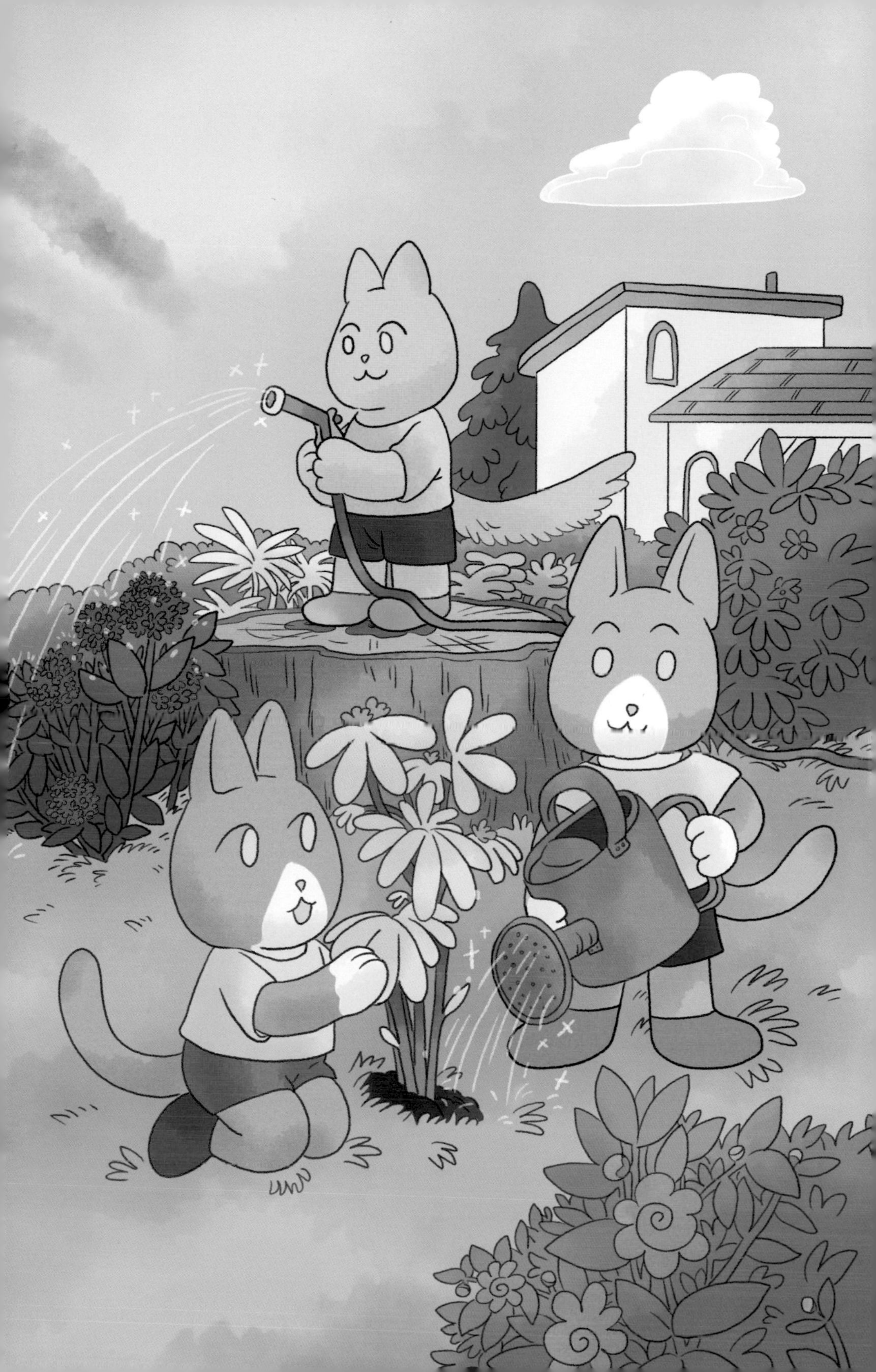

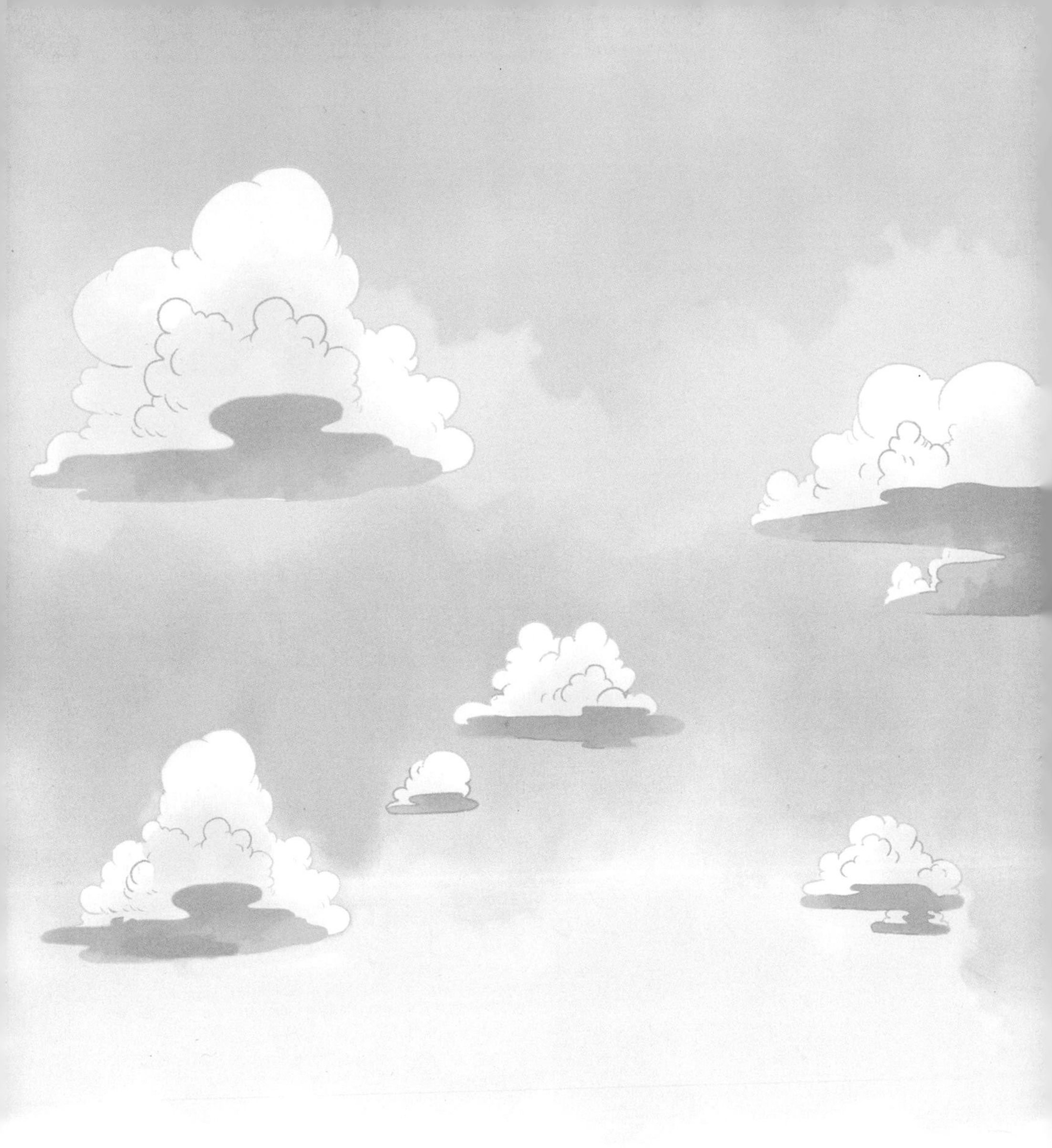

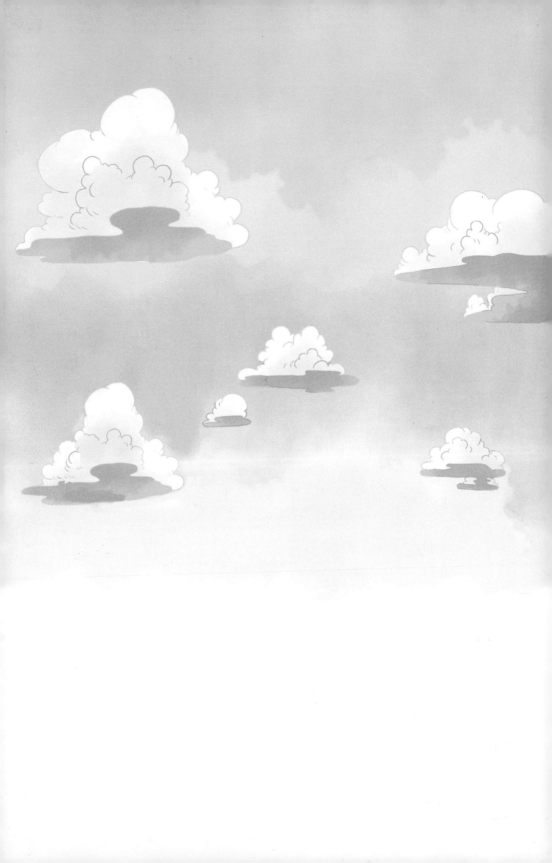